D1020112

The Jew of Home Depot and Other Stories

Johns Hopkins: Poetry and Fiction
John T. Irwin, General Editor

Max Apple

The Jew of Home Depot

and Other Stories

THE JOHNS HOPKINS UNIVERSITY PRESS
Baltimore

The author thanks the editors in whose publications the following stories first appeared: "Yao's Chick," *The Atlantic;* "Indian Giver," *Story;* "Stabbing an Elephant," National Public Radio's *Chanukah Lights;* "Peace," *Harper's Magazine;* "Stepdaughters," *Esquire;* "Sized Up," *Boston Globe Magazine;* "Threads," *Testimony;* "House of the Lowered," *Maggid;* "Strawberry Shortcake," *Witness;* "Adventures in Dementia," *Fiction;* "Talker," *Fiction;* and "The Jew of Home Depot," *The Hopkins Review.*

This book has been brought to publication with the generous assistance of the G. Harry Pouder Fund.

Publication of this book is supported in part by an award from the National Endowment for the Arts.

 Published 2007
Printed in the United States of America on acid-free paper
2 4 6 8 9 7 5 3 1

The Johns Hopkins University Press
2715 North Charles Street
Baltimore, Maryland 21218-4363
www.press.jhu.edu

Library of Congress Cataloging-in-Publication Data

Apple, Max.
The Jew of Home Depot and other stories / Max Apple.
p. cm.
ISBN-13: 978-0-8018-8738-3 (acid-free paper)
ISBN-10: 0-8018-8738-0 (acid-free paper)
I. Title.
PS3551.P56J49 2007
813'.54—dc22 2007018864

A catalog record for this book is available from the British Library.

Special discounts are available for bulk purchases of this book. For more information, please contact Special Sales at 410-516-6936 or specialsales@press.jhu.edu for Talya

Contents

The Jew of Home Depot and Other Stories

Yao's Chick

THE FAMILY watched basketball in order to enjoy the Rockets' new Chinese player. They took pride in him the way they would have taken pride in a Chinese astronaut or a new high-tech millionaire. Li En, sitting between her parents, tried to pretend that she wasn't really paying attention to the TV. She looked mostly down at a needlepoint cat in its frame.

"This Mr. Moochie needs a haircut," her father said. "Look at him; he looks like he's been in a tornado."

"He's Moochie," Li En corrected, "not Mr. Moochie."

"What kind of the name is that?" her father asked. "Is it American?"

"Yes," Li En said. Then she reminded him that most Americans thought Yao was a funny name.

Her father raised his eyebrows; he specialized at keeping his body still in the midst of movement. He went to the window where he could look out at her fourteen-year-old twin brothers, Tommy and Timmy, as they practiced on the trampoline in their driveway. Her father didn't have to call out any instructions. Li En and her brothers could read his mantra in his eyes: "Elbows against ribs, kneecaps at lips, chin on chest."

Until she grew too tall and too old, Li En had also practiced as much as three hours a day. At twelve, the high point of her life, she had won the Texas girls "Best Overall" trophy. On that day at the Memorial Coliseum in Dallas, while the judges observed, her father took the trophy from her dry hands and held it aloft. He closed his eyes as if in prayer. The judges lowered their heads to join him. It looked as if he pointed the tip of the trophy toward downtown Dallas, but he aimed much further east. "We showed the fucking Communists," he whispered to his daughter. When he placed the trophy back in her hands, it no longer felt like it belonged to her.

Even now, twenty-seven years after he'd escaped from Saigon on the day that the Communists torched his gymnastics academy, her father was still showing them, although he had changed instruments, from Li En to his twin sons, with whom he roamed the southwest gathering trophies. At church, and even in the neighborhood, people had begun to call Li En "Auntie" because she was twelve years older and so much taller than her brothers. She and her parents were Chinese immigrants from Vietnam; her brothers were just plain old Texans.

Her father returned to the couch when the third quarter started. "I don't think they need so many players," he said, "just one to throw the ball to Yao. And I think if he knew that there would be no second opportunities he would not miss so many times."

Li En had respect but no love for her father. She had not forgiven him for dropping her training when she passed five foot eight. "You should specialize in something else," he said, and he insisted that she go to junior college and study computers. When she shot past six feet he became embarrassed by her size and sent her mother to Mr. Feng, the card reader who lived above the dollar store on South Main Street.

Mr. Feng said the reason for Li En's unusual height was the inauspicious hour of her conception. He told her mother, "You were in flight, your business lay in ruin, Granny sat in the boat beside you coughing up blood, pirates roamed the South China Sea, and still you and your husband, at such a moment, created a child."

In her defense Li En's mother told the card reader that they were not trying to create a child. "I just wanted to keep him alive. He kept saying he wished he had stayed with his academy. He was screaming, 'If I didn't burn, let me drown.' He said he was going into the water. I placed my body on top of his trying to keep him from the Gulf of Thailand."

"You are fortunate," the card reader told her mother, "Li En is merely tall. This is not so bad."

"It makes it difficult for her to marry," her mother said.

"Perhaps I can be of assistance," the card reader said.

Li En refused his help. She also refused to accompany her father and brothers to Lake Charles, Louisiana, where her father wanted once more to include her in a competition. "You can catch," he said, "Timmy on one shoulder, Tommy on the other. Then we will have a killer dismount. As you somersault forward, the boys will do backflips from your shoulders. This will win first prize in family category," her father said.

Li En did not want this kind of family category. She wanted to start her own family. She was twenty-six and without prospects. At church her mother prayed, and at Crystal Nail, where she lacquered and lengthened, her mother asked customers about eligible young men. She kept Li En's graduation photo mounted in the right corner of her mirror so that every customer would see her daughter, diploma in hand.

As they watched the game, Li En could hardly stand to see so many players pull at Yao and raise their hands in front of his face whenever he tried to shoot for the basket. She could tell how polite he was by the way he shook his head in apology whenever he allowed someone to take the ball from him.

"This is a strange game," her father said. "There is no holding any muscles in position, no somersaulting; only jumping and throwing a ball. Without a ball it would be far better." When he left the living room to turn off the outdoor spotlight and call the boys in for bed, Li En's mother squeezed her daughter's hand. Since the Yu San episode, her mother had been treating her like someone under a death sentence.

"What are you thinking?" Li En asked.

"I'm thinking of how I nursed you when you were a baby in the refugee camp in Thailand."

"Is that a happy memory for you?"

"Yes," her mother said, "very happy. My sister would sit with us; she was the age you are now and she was already a widow with four children."

"Please," Li En said, "I've heard enough of these kinds of happy stories. Doesn't this family have any really happy stories? Didn't we have picnics or go on vacations or go fishing? Why is it always war and vengeance?"

Her mother changed her position on the couch to face her daughter. "You think because you are educated that you know everything. War and suffering is also education."

"Do you want me to suffer?" Li En asked. "Okay, I'm suffering."

"No, no," her mother said, "I want you to marry and be happy and continue your good career at Progressive Data, and I will help with the children."

Li En did not answer. What was there to say?

Tears came to her mother's eyes. "Oh mama, stop," Li En said, "it wasn't your fault."

"It was my fault," her mother said, "I created this disappointment."

In a way she had. Almost daily she talked at Crystal Nail about her large daughter who was so fussy that she wouldn't agree to meet a young man who was not tall enough to look into her eyes. Mrs. Chuk, having her nails done at another station, overheard and said that her son was the tallest Chinese boy at Texas Tech, and so it began. Mrs. Chuk switched stations and every few weeks, when she came in for nailwork, they talked about Yu San and the possibilities of a match. Li En learned, at second hand, so much about the young man. He was an honor student but didn't like to study. They loved Yu San at Texas Tech, but it was so windy in Lubbock and he missed his family. Then he had a girlfriend and disappeared from the conversation at Crystal Nail. But when he broke up with the girl, his mother said he would be back home at the end of the semester. Then Texas Tech kept offering him scholarships to stay there. Then, finally, he did come home and saved Texas Tech $12,000. His mother promised that he would call Li En at any minute, and three months after that warning he did call.

"Hey," he said, "I know we're supposed to meet, you know, from our moms." He suggested the Red Lobster, "the one near Target." He told her that she could call him Earl. He didn't mention his height, but he said that he drove a maroon Corolla. "I'll pick you up at seven. If you can, wait outside. I hate to circle around for parking when it's just a quick stop."

When he drove up, exactly on time, Li En could see even before they greeted each other that his head grazed the Toyota's ceiling. "Tech sucks," he said, "but U of H sucks too." He said "bingo" when he found a parking spot directly in front of Red Lobster. While they waited for their meal, Earl took out his Game Boy. When he did something good with his thumbs he held out the screen to show Li En. "You want a turn?" he asked.

Li En understood that this was her marriage opportunity. While he ate steamed crab and soup and salad, she let herself imagine spending the rest of her life with Earl. He had clean fingernails and small ears that were close to his skull. She could see him, not too many years from now, playing computer games with their children. He was certainly tall enough and he didn't slouch. When the waitress brought the check he divided it equally. "Is that okay with you?" he asked.

"Yes," she said, and it was more than okay, it was exactly okay, it was fifty-fifty, a partnership. A week later he invited her to the Red Lobster again, and then, during a lull in a nail wrapping, his mother told her mother that Earl Yu San wanted to have twenty-five thousand dollars in the bank and be a department manager before he chose a wife. And he was only twenty-three. After work her mother consulted Mr. Feng. She then reported to her daughter in a bitter tone, almost a chant, "The three-year difference is the most unlucky number. Mr. Feng says that you should stay away from Yu San or there will be catastrophes, early deaths, poverty, crippled children."

"I don't believe in your stupid fortune-teller," Li En said. "Stop telling me what he says; I don't care what he says." When Yu San didn't call her again, Li En blamed her mother and Mr. Feng.

"Not so," her mother said, "I never told his mother anything. I just do her nails now and all we talk about is nails. That's all. And he still has two more years to become an engineer. This is not because of Mr. Feng. This is the blame of jobs and colleges.

After another month of silence, Li En called Earl Yu San. She tried to sound happy and girlish and indifferent. "So," she said, "what about Red Lobster?"

"Can't," he said, 'I've got midterms and a lot of stuff going on. You know."

Li En sobbed for half an hour. Her mother stroked her hair.

"I know that I caused you this heartache. I ask your forgiveness. Please," she said, "open your heart to Mr. Feng."

"Are you going to tell this to Mr. Feng too?"

"I already did. Who else can I tell, your father?"

When she had recovered enough from the experience to consider her mother's wishes, Li En walked the extra six blocks from the bus stop to the fortune-teller's office. She read the business card thumbtacked to his door: "Leon Feng—Interpreter and Counselor." She expected an old person, but the man who greeted her at the door, apart from a scattering of gray hairs, seemed surprisingly youthful. In painters trousers and a Hawaiian shirt, he looked like a middle-aged man who had won a shopping trip to Gap Kids, the name on his sneakers. He led her to a plastic lawn chair in what seemed to be his living room, dining room, and office. An IBM electric typewriter and a rice cooker sat side by side on his table. "I am here only because of my mother," Li En said. He smiled and looked serious at the same time.

"I understand this. Do you prefer to speak English?"

"Yes," she said, "and I would also prefer for my mother and you to please respect my privacy."

"Of course," he said, "I only wish to be of help. Is there some service I can do for you?"

"You can stop telling my mother that I was conceived in an inauspicious hour."

He lowered his eyes. "I'm very sorry," he said. "I know this must be a problem."

"Not for me," Li En said, "but you make my mother sad." He nodded. "Why do you tell her such things? Why do you seal my fate?"

"I do no such thing," Mr. Feng said. "I only advise on specific matters. Your mother asked me once, 'Should I buy a refrigerator with ice cube tray.' I said no. If you lack ice, perhaps this is my fault."

"You know what I lack," Li En said. She rose to her full height so that Mr. Feng had to look up and expose his Adam's apple to her judgmental eyes. She was ready to leave, but after making the effort to see him she also wanted him to tell her something, maybe a recipe, a secret phrase, a type of perfume, the name of a singles service—she wouldn't act on anything he said, but she still wanted to hear something, she wanted to come away with an assignment. She sat down.

"Well," Li En asked, "are you going to tell me what to do?"

"This is possible," Mr. Feng said. "The fee will be fifteen dollars." Li En laughed to cover her anger.

"So, you are just like everyone else," she said. "My mother's fortune-teller hero is just like the dentist and the dry cleaner."

"Yes," he said, "deliverer of services."

Li En reached for her purse. She would take the money out of what she paid her father for rent. She would tell him, "female needs." If he could take days off work to travel with the boys, he could pay for Mr. Feng. She handed the interpreter three fives.

"Very very good," Mr. Feng said. "And rare. Most people have a $20 bill and they need change, or they give me 10, and 5, or one $10 bill and five ones. But three 5s—this is the best possible. Do you require a receipt?"

"No," she said, "I require advice about marriage."

Mr. Feng held up his hands, looked at them himself, then presented all ten fingers to Li En. "No ring of marriage," he said. "I have not had that good fortune myself."

"Then how can you advise others?"

"This is a problem," he said. "Most of the time I give advice on financial matters or cultural misunderstanding. Can you return next week? This will give me time to consult sources and books."

Li En rose again, this time to leave, not to intimidate. "I don't think I need your advice," she said. On the way out she stopped at the dollar store and bought her mother a card full of colorful hairpins.

Her family didn't take the newspaper. The boys could care less about news and her parents practiced their reading just as well on free neighborhood weeklies. Li En started to buy the *Houston Chronicle* at the bus stop. First she looked for photos of Yao Ming and then she scanned the pages for his name. She didn't know what the letters and numbers in the box score meant but she understood that higher numbers were better for him and she took great pride in seeing them. She wanted to go to a game but felt embarrassed to tell her mother and once more involve her parent in private matters. In January she lied. "On Tuesday there will be a benefit honoring Mr. Lerner," she said, and her mother suggested, as Li En knew she would, that her daughter wear the red silk dress that Mrs. Wang had made especially for such occasions.

"It's going to be casual," she told her mother.

"For you casual," her mother said. "For Mr. Lerner, it's very important." Her mother offered to make a floral arrangement for Mr. Lerner's table.

"Stop it," Li En yelled, angry at herself for lying and at her mother for making it take on so much importance.

"I'll just be home late, that's all."

On Tuesday, the day of the Rockets-Wolves game, Li En felt sick to her stomach. By noon she had to leave work. She still hoped to be able to attend the game, but when her mother came in from Crystal Nail at three, a half-hour before the twins returned from school, Li En told her mother everything. Then she vomited and had chills. Her mother gave her a hot-water bottle and the feather comforter that they rarely needed in Texas. She slept fitfully throughout the evening. When her mother checked on her at eleven, just after father left for the nightshift at Happy Doughnut, her mother whispered in Chinese the score of the game, "Rocket 101, Timberwolf 97."

"Plural," Li En said. "They're all more than one."

"Okay," her mother said, "but only one matters."

The following day she still felt weak and dizzy. Her mother had left her some soup in the refrigerator, and Li En was relaxing on the couch as she watched ESPN Classics when Mr. Feng made a house call.

"Please excuse me," she told him when she answered the door, "I don't feel very good."

"I understand," he said, "and I'm sorry to disturb you. I will only stay a minute." His eyes lingered on the TV, where the 1984 Super Bowl was being replayed. From a plastic bag he withdrew a box of chocolate-covered cherries and a small purple plant. He put them on the kitchen table. "I hope you are better very soon."

Because of his gifts she felt obliged to play hostess, even briefly. "Would you like some tea? Forgive me for being dressed like this."

"I should be asking forgiveness for arriving without warning," he said, "and your dressing gown is very lovely. Is it also made for you by Mrs. Wang?"

"Oh God," Li En said, "is there anything my mother hasn't told you? No—I bought this at JCPenney's. Do you want to know the size and the price? Do you need the sales receipt?"

Mr. Feng turned pale. She thought his hand shook and she regretted showing him so much temper. The fortune-teller was a busybody, no doubt about that, but he probably intended no harm. She should be angry at her mother, not at him. She swore to herself that she would never again confide in her mother.

"Don't trouble yourself to make tea," he said.

"It's no trouble; we have boiling water in the hot pot." She pointed to the counter.

"If you don't mind then," Mr. Feng said, "I'll have coffee." He reached into his pocket for an aluminum single-serve packet of instant and a companion packet of creamer. He smiled proudly. "Dollar store," he said.

At the kitchen table, with the steam from his coffee cup fogging his large glasses, Mr. Feng made himself comfortable.

"Do you have many clients?" Li En asked.

"Some weeks are better than others. Your mother is my most steady customer."

"If I may ask, how do you make a living at your job? I mean how many people these days go to a card reader rather than to a psychologist?"

"Many," he said, "although it's true that Westerners prefer astrology and palm reading. But it has been my good fortune to live where I do. If I have even one client each week I can easily buy milk and bread and beef jerky and peanut butter and I never lack for a great variety of cheeses and sweets and frozen pizza bites."

"I get it," she said.

"The dollar store is a wonderful American institution; there everything truly is equal. And evenings, after 9 PM it is my pleasure to sweep and mop the floors and tidy the shelves. For this service I receive free rent."

"So you can live on almost nothing?"

"Almost."

"And you're happy about this?"

"Yes," he said, "who wouldn't be?"

Li En stopped herself. If he was happy about living that way let him be happy.

"Are you a sports fan?" he asked.

"I'm sure my mother has told you about my interest in basketball."

Mr. Feng nodded, and when Li En blushed he put his lips to his coffee cup and stayed in that position until she chose to speak again.

"As long as you're here," she said, "do you have any advice about this matter of sports?"

"I do," Mr. Feng said. It was clear that he was only waiting to be asked. He pulled a sheet of lined paper from his pocket and stood as he read aloud, the way a child would in a school play.

"I have consulted the I Ching and also the writings of a psychologist from the capital of Sweden. Both advise the same thing." Mr. Feng raised his hand with his fist in the air. "Go for it," he said loudly. Li En noticed that his eyes, though no longer fogged by steam, still seemed clouded. He waited a moment for his advice to sink in. "Okay," he said, "all good wishes for your recovery from illness."

He bowed his head slightly and backed away from her toward the door. Li En, pleased in spite of her skepticism by his energetic advice, luxuriated for a moment before she ran to the door and called out to Mr. Feng, who was already at the bottom of the iron staircase. "Do I owe you fifteen dollars for this?"

"No," he said as he turned to face her, "the original fee paid for this research."

The next home game was Thursday, Utah Jazz. Li En told her mother in an offhand and icy way that she would be home late, nothing else. At the box office window a woman with the face of a dog told her, "Sold out." When Li En didn't understand, the woman pointed to a sign.

"But I only want one ticket," Li En said.

"Sorry," the lady said, "next time why don't you call first and charge your ticket, then you can go straight to the will-call window."

Li En turned away from the box office. People singly and in groups were approaching the arena from all angles, even from underground. Watching entire families and people bouncing with anticipation emerge from the parking tunnel made her think of the risen dead on the day of salvation.

"I've got three in section 112," a black man with a goatee whispered in her ear as he held the tickets literally in front of her eyes. "Nine rows behind the iron, the seat to beat at dunk time."

"I only want one ticket," Li En said.

"One is better than none, slip me 75 and in section 112 you arrive."

Li En handed him four 20s and he plucked her change from a wad of bills in his front pocket. "Enjoy the game," he said as he walked away from her holding his two remaining tickets in the air.

While she watched the game Li En tried to be interested in all the players, but she kept her eyes only on Yao Ming. She liked best when he wasn't playing. Then she could look at him sitting on the bench and imagine him at home relaxing in a chair especially elongated for him as he read the Chinese paper while she prepared his supper. After dinner she would help with his English, and if his mother wanted to live with them, that would be all the better. She knew that he earned millions of dollars but she would continue to work because you could never trust the government of China to actually let him keep that money.

During a time-out she was staring at the bench and hardly noticed the roar of the crowd, but when the chant began she looked away from the resting Yao to the middle of the floor. "Turbo, Turbo," the crowd chanted, and she spotted a creature dressed head to toe in a blue and silver suit. He held a basketball in his right hand and raced toward the basket in front of her. At the free-throw line, his feet hit a 3' × 3' trampoline exactly in stride, and he executed as perfect a somersault as Li En had ever seen. On his way down he dropped in the ball and the crowd went wild. People cheered far more than they had for Yao Ming. Turbo walked to the center of the floor, raised his arm in triumph, and ran away. When the players returned Li En was still holding her breath.

The acrobat performed twice more, the second time doing an incredible backward somersault on his way to the basket. She had no idea that these things happened at basketball games. They never showed this on television. Now she understood why people paid so much to see the games in person. She knew that her father would find much to criticize in Turbo's form. She could hear him say that real judges would never give points for his approach and landing and maybe just a few for the actual somersault. But this audience was not interested in form, only in the astounding ways he found to throw the basketball into the hole.

Yao Ming rested all of the last quarter because the Rockets were far ahead, and by the time the game ended, half the crowd had already left. Li En waited until her aisle was entirely clear, then she walked toward the basketball floor, where ushers in dark blue vests were now guarding the empty playing area. One of the ushers stopped her at the edge of the floor.

"Sorry," he said, "you need a pass to get beyond here."

"I want to see Yao Ming," she said in Mandarin as she looked down at the man's baldness. The fact that he understood nothing that she said made him seem more interested in her.

"Are you a relative?"

Li En minced no words, in Mandarin she told the truth, "I hope to become his wife." The usher made a sign for her to wait as he conferred with a nearby policeman, then he waved her toward the tunnel underneath the arena, the one she'd seen the players use. Li En had no plan; she allowed her heart to tell her mouth what to say, and though the usher did not know the words he must have understood her meaning. "I will only tell the truth," she said to herself, "I will not be ashamed to say who I am and why I am here."

The tunnel led to a long hallway, where she took her place standing against the wall across from the players' locker room. She knew this was the right place because many women stood there, beautiful women whose clothing made Li En realize that she should have dressed in Mrs. Wang's red dress instead of the gray slacks and ivory blouse and tennis shoes that she wore to the office and then to the game.

"You waiting for Yao?" A black woman asked her.

"Yes," she said. As Taisha introduced herself, Li En felt so unglamorous, so out of place, that she barely dared to touch the friendly woman's outstretched hand. Then from the doorway the players began to emerge, one after another, so tall and handsome, some wearing gold necklaces, most in suits that shimmered with silk. They looked like princes from the drawings in the books her mother used to read to her. As each player walked out she would have liked to have them introduced once more as they had been so wonderfully named before the game, but they needed no introduction to their waiting friends. Taisha introduced her to Moochie.

"She's Yao's chick," Taisha said.

"Hey, Yao's chick," Moochie said as he shook her hand.

Li En waited until all the players and their friends left the hallway. Then she continued to wait. There was no noise along the corridor, not from the Rockets' dressing room or from the visitors' room at the opposite end of the hallway. She heard no sounds from the sixteen thousand seats in the arena above her. Finally the Rockets' door opened and a janitor wearing a Rockets cap backward emerged. He pulled a large canvas cart loaded with uniforms.

"Excuse me," Li En said, "I am waiting for Yao Ming. He has not come out."

"He leaves from the back, goes straight to the garage," the man said. "He gets into his limo and the driver . . ." He made a sign with his hand to signify speeding away. "It's a circus every time Yao comes out, so he does all his interviews in the afternoon, just before pregame snack."

"Then he won't come out here like the other players?"

"Never does," the man said. He pushed his canvas cart down the corridor. "You better hustle. They must have locked most of the exits by now."

Li En had to push herself away from the wall where she had been standing. When she looked at her watch she realized that she'd been waiting for an hour and a half.

She imagined Yao Ming at home, resting while his mother rubbed liniment into the shoulder he'd fallen on during the game. While she had been waiting in the hallway outside the locker room of Compaq Center, Yao had probably been examining his feet, all red and swollen from so much jumping and stopping and starting. Her own feet felt heavy as she walked up the dark tunnel where, a few hours before, fans had leaned over the edge, almost falling from the stands in order get a closer look at Yao and his fellow players. She had already turned away from the basketball floor and was walking toward the only red exit sign still lit when she heard the sound of a ball going through the basket. In the deserted arena it sounded like a whip. She turned to see Turbo. He stood in the middle of the floor, he pawed the ground like a horse, then he sped toward the basket, hit the trampoline, and did a double somersault. He had no ball; instead, he hung from the orange iron for a few seconds. Li En saw that he had placed a small trampoline in front of each basket, and at mid court he had his own canvas cart loaded with basketballs. He practices after the games she thought, maybe has a regular job during the day and this is his only opportunity.

Impulsively, Li En turned toward the floor; her legs took over and she began to run. She had not done a straight approach in a judged event for many years, but from time to time she still practiced with her brothers and she knew the feel of the trampoline as well as the feel of her tongue. She did a simple somersault and landing. The surprised Turbo clapped his encased hands. Then he ran toward her, led her by the fingertips to his cart full of basketballs, and placed one in her hands.

"Can you do a somersault with the ball?" He asked.

Li En shook her head. "I have to keep my elbows against my ribs as I've been taught."

Turbo began to laugh, "And you keep your knees close to your mouth, right?"

"Yes," Li En said.

"You're an old-fashioned girl," Turbo said. "Everything is changed now." His voice from behind the spandex mask sounded distant but friendly. "Try holding the ball, try a running dunk. It will be easy for you." He tossed her a small basketball.

It felt so odd for Li En to hold the ball. She concentrated on moving her elbows away from her ribs. "My father would not approve," she said. She stretched her arms. Turbo laughed again and bounced the ball that he held in his hands.

"Dunk it," he said. Li En ran holding the ball in front of her. She felt like a bird carrying an egg. Her feet hit the trampoline in stride. On her way down she pushed the ball through with two hands. Under the basket, she landed with her arms stretched, her legs wide as if waiting for the judges approval.

"Yao couldn't do that and Shaq couldn't either and Kobe—maybe," Turbo said. "You've got the moves."

Li En rolled the ball back toward the masked gymnast. "See you," Turbo called out. "Keep practicing."

Outside in the chilled January air, she saw no players and no fans. She had already turned toward the bus stop when she noticed Mr. Feng waiting near another exit. He ran toward her. "Your mother called me because she was worried," he said.

"There's nothing to worry about," Li En said, "the Rockets won easily."

"May I accompany you home?" Mr. Feng asked. "The No. 66 bus runs until midnight. She noticed that he wore leather shoes and a Rockets jacket. They walked a few steps in silence. "I hope that my advice has been useful to you," he said.

Li En had some soreness in her left calf and she felt embarrassed about how her hair must look after the somersaults. She walked quickly but the fortune-teller, though his head barely reached her shoulder, matched her stride for stride with brisk steps. At the bus stop, beneath the lighted billboard of Yao Ming, they waited. Li En considered gymnastics and basketball and the hour of her birth. When the bus arrived, she decided to ask Mr. Feng what he thought might happen next.

Indian Giver

At first, Seymour Rubin thought his new employee was practicing voodoo—later he understood that it was only cleanliness. The tall goateed black man stood on top of the baler using a broomstick. Vinnie, the crane operator, held the 1,500-pound steel magnet in midair above him while Alonzo Johnson poked his stick into the partly crushed body of a '74 Pontiac and came up with something.

Seymour, looking out his office window, came running to save a life. By the time he reached the baler Alonzo had jumped off the machine. He held his catch, a wad of dark threads, under Seymour's nose. "It's the cord from radial tires," Alonzo said. "That's what clogs your baler. And this too." From his pocket he pulled a few ounces of cotton batting.

"It's from the car seats. You got to pluck this shit out. It's poison to your machine."

After that first time Seymour learned to trust him. Alonzo took care of the machine the way Seymour looked after his son, Chuckie. On Saturday, his day off, Alonzo came in to clean the baler. The manual specified no maintenance but Alonzo knew better. He crawled right into the motor housing and squirted lubricants from a long-nosed can directly onto the gear teeth. Lying on his back he tested the belt pressure with his hands, and with his breath he blew dirt from the hydraulic lifts.

Every Christmas Seymour gave him a $500 bonus, but you couldn't pay the man enough to equal his worth. Because of Alonzo, Seymour's

Salvage after thirty-five so-so years in Muskegon, Michigan, began to show solid profits. Steel prices stayed up and the baler operated better than it ever had.

The car buffs who knew Seymour's Salvage thought he made a living from the twenty-five-dollar transmissions and the forty-dollar motor blocks they bought, but on them he barely broke even. For profit he needed to produce the one-ton bundles that the baler made of car bodies. As the baler went, so went Seymour's Salvage.

On the terrible Friday when Seymour learned the truth, he was on his way to the baler room to deliver two decks of plastic-coated playing cards to the yardmen. At lunchtime they wolfed down their sandwiches in five minutes, then sat, like millionaires, on leather bucket seats playing seven card stud.

When Seymour walked in nobody was playing poker. Lamont Thomas and Willie Boyd and James Winston and the brothers Hal and Dean Smith sat in their car seats with their heads bowed. Alonzo stood in front of them, his eyes closed.

"Allah," Alonzo said, "help us to understand the words of our leaders. Help us to get the Jew off our back and punish him as he deserves."

"Amen," the yard workers answered, and Seymour, standing at the door, couldn't believe what he heard. He stood still for a few seconds until his voice came to him.

"What's going on?" he asked.

Alonzo opened his eyes.

"We were praying, Seymour." he said. "You shouldn't interrupt praying."

"Is my baler room a church?"

"On Fridays from twelve to one," Alonzo said. "It is a mosque. We pray and the men don't bring no pork in their lunches. Little by little they're learning."

"What are they learning, to hate me?"

"Not you," the baler operator said. "I told everyone at the beginning that the Jew is not Seymour Rubin. You ain't responsible for your people, Seymour."

"How long has this been going on," Seymour asked, "your once a week anti-Semitism?"

"We been praying and talking together almost a year," Alonzo said. "The Jew is only one of our topics."

"I should have known," Seymour said, "when you started all that Muslim business, all those *Salam Alekhams.* I should have known you were my enemy."

Seymour picked up the sledgehammer that Alonzo kept near the door. "Out!" he yelled. The yardmen left, Alonzo kept his ground.

"You're through forever," Seymour yelled. He pointed to the door.

"If I go," Alonzo said, "who'll run the baler?"

"Out," Seymour yelled again. He raised the sledgehammer.

Alonzo, far from the door, backed around the 9' × 12' baler room. When he reached the door he ran. His youth and longer strides barely got him to the parking lot ahead of Seymour. Alonzo's Mercury burned rubber just as Seymour aimed the twelve-pound hammer at the car's trunk. Seymour fell to his knees, then grabbed at his groin.

"Thank God I didn't see it," his wife Phyllis said later. "He grabbed himself, then he yelled, 'Phyllis, help!' One of the yardmen drove him to the hospital."

There, too, Seymour was surrounded by anti-Semites.

"You're crazy," Phyllis said, "the orderlies are not the Germans, and this is Muskegon, Michigan, not Nazi Germany."

Seymour didn't answer. When he started to get excited it hurt too much in his abdomen. The fresh stitches were themselves a reminder that the hernia happened because he decided to fight.

"You're a seventy-year-old man," Phyllis said. "What you need is a long vacation. I'm not talking about nine days in Miami Beach or seven days cooped up in a hotel in Jerusalem at some UJA conference. I'm talking about a place with sunshine and exotic fruits."

"You want a cruise," Seymour mumbled, "go on a cruise. To me a vacation is watching a World Series game, then going to the yard in the morning."

"That's why you are what you are," Phyllis said. "You're in the hospital and mad at everybody."

"I'm mad at liars and at Jew-baiters."

"You're mad at your son and at your best worker. What are you all of a sudden, a saint, a protector of the Jewish people?"

"You're damned right I am," Seymour said. "A protector of the Jewish people, and Jewish land, and even Jewish trees, and you would be too if you didn't listen to Sonny Boy's opinions like he was some Walter Cronkite."

"Don't start on Chuckie, don't blame the hernia on him. He didn't tell you to pick up a sledgehammer. He's in Arizona helping people."

"The wrong people," Seymour said. "Indians. He should be on a kibbutz, protecting it from Arabs, or he should be here, helping me fight off the black anti-Semites."

"God forbid," Phyllis said. She handed Seymour a card.

"Chuckie sent this."

Seymour looked at a drawing of little hands holding pink and orange flowers. On the bottom Chuckie had signed "Get well soon, Dad. Joyce sends her love, too."

Seymour had yet to meet Chuckie's girlfriend, but he had seen a photograph of Joyce Van Damm on the reservation. In the picture she stood next to an Indian woman who was smoking a pipe. Joyce had to bend her head so that you could see her. She looked like a giraffe, and the Indian woman with blankets and pipe looked to Seymour like an Indian man.

Seymour turned the card over. "UNICEF," he said. "I thought so. Also anti-Semites."

"It's not UNICEF that's anti-Semites," Phyllis told her recuperating husband. "That's UNESCO. UNICEF helps children."

"Arab children," Seymour said. "I wouldn't give you a nickel for the whole UN."

Phyllis stood firm. "UNICEF helps poor children throughout the world, Arabs too. Why shouldn't they?"

"Who helped the Jewish children? Who helped my cousin Tzi at Treblinka? Where was UNICEF?"

"Seymour, be reasonable. There was no UNICEF then. Not even the UN. You know that."

"I'll be reasonable," Seymour said, "when my son is reasonable. When Yassar Arafat is reasonable. When Alonzo Johnson is reasonable."

"Please," said Phyllis, "not now, not this. You're a sick man. You're recovering from major surgery. You should talk hospital talk."

"All right," Seymour said. "Hospital talk. My temperature is 98.6.

My blood pressure is 140/90. My urine trickles out. My bowels I already forgot."

"Enough," Phyllis said. "Let's talk about getting well and taking a trip."

"I'm not going anyplace," Seymour said, "until the Nazis are out of Muskegon."

An orderly walked in carrying a tray.

"Dinner," the young man said. "You've got semisoft. Let's see, that's Jell-O, and soup with crackers, and an omelette. Looks good.

"You're a Black Muslim?" Seymour asked.

The orderly put down the tray. "No," he said, "why do you ask?"

"It's on my mind," Seymour said. "I learned that one of my friends, a black man who I treated like family, thinks that Louis Farakhan is right."

"Who's Louis Farakhan?"

"A leader of your people. An anti-Semite. A dangerous man. A Hitler lover."

"Take it easy, man." The orderly eased Seymour's legs back onto the bed. "You stay in bed and have your supper. Then once you get stronger you go give hell to whoever he is."

"You've got to excuse my husband," Phyllis said. "He's recovering."

"I'm fine."

"You bet," the orderly said. "And you'll be even better after you eat." He walked to the door.

"You're all right," Seymour said. "When you need parts for your car come see me. Seymour's Salvage."

"That you?" The black man smiled. "I bought a universal joint at your place. So you're Seymour. You got some parts yard there."

"Next time you come, ask for me. I'll give you a good price."

"You bet I will. See you later, Seymour."

"That's what I like to see," Phyllis said, "friendly talk. Like you used to make to everyone."

"I'm friendly," Seymour said, "to my friends, not to my enemies."

"Stop being so edgy, and maybe you'll remember who your friends are." She held up a notice from the hospital. "Alonzo donated blood for you."

"Throw it away," Seymour said.

She put the paper in the trash basket.

"I mean the blood," Seymour said.

"If he's such an enemy," Phyllis asked, "why did he come to give blood?"

"Guilt," Seymour said. "Blacks also know what it means."

Before he could return to work Seymour's baler broke down twice. The first was a minor clog that the yardmen fixed in an afternoon. The second was a torn bushing in the motor. The part alone cost four thousand dollars and Seymour had to bring in a mechanic from Milwaukee to install it.

Phyllis didn't want him to get too excited.

"Just thank God that you're okay," she said. "The doctor says you'll be as good as new. Don't get yourself worked up about the baler."

"I made a choice," he said. "I'd rather have baler trouble than a Hitler in my yard. I'm not worried about the cost."

Phyllis thought her husband's new attitude was a pleasant side effect of the anesthesia.

Seymour recovered quickly. Only ten days after the surgery, the doctor allowed him to go down to his basement for a little recreation. There Seymour had a workshop. A welder since he was eighteen, in his late years he had turned his first job into a hobby. When Chuckie went away to college and the house was so empty you could cry, Seymour brought a small torch and a few door panels home from the yard and began to weld. At first he just made geometric shapes and tried to keep his welding spots as neat as possible. Then, as he got reacquainted with his old trade, he began to make objects and people. For some reason everything he made was Jewish. Old men with earlocks, welded scrolls, menorahs and mezuzahs, two-handled hand-washing cups and smaller ones for dipping fingernails only. He made Seder plates and steel challahs, and round welded bagels covered with strips of gray lox. The wooden shelves in his basement were filled with Seymour's handiwork.

A regular Jewish museum, Phyllis called it. She wanted to take up a few items and display them on the coffee table but her husband refused.

"You're an artist," she said. "If you'd let me advertise a little, people would call you with special orders for bar mitzvahs and weddings."

"It's a hobby, that's all. I've got welding. Our son has Indians."

"Enough," Phyllis said, "don't put your bitterness about the shop on our son's shoulders."

Three weeks after he swung the sledgehammer and ruptured his abdomen, Seymour Rubin returned to work. In his absence, and Alonzo's, a mountain of junk four hundred cars high grew beside the baler. Lamont McCoy, the new baler operator, almost got killed trying to do Alonzo's job. Lamont climbed up to pluck a tire from the crusher with Alonzo's stick, but he forgot to signal first and Vinnie dropped an '88 van a foot from his head.

"I thought it was Jesus," Lamont said, "when that old Dodge went whooooosh in my ear like an airplane."

Lamont wanted no more of the baler. He returned to the yard where he had experience knocking radiators loose from motor blocks.

Other workers took their turns. It didn't matter who, once or twice a week the machine clogged and it took all day to clean it. And much worse, the big repairs came like an epidemic and ate up more than the profits.

After the first four thousand dollars Seymour took no moral pleasure in the breakdowns. The first was honor, the rest were ruining him. The gear teeth twisted, the hydraulic arm decayed, the crusher door collapsed. Each time the machine was down for weeks, and cost thousands to repair.

Five months after his operation, Seymour had to borrow money from the Michigan National Bank just to meet his payroll for the ten men and Helen, the office girl. His entire cash flow, the old cars, sat unbaled beside the machine. There were so many of them that the car hulks clogged the aisles and kept customers from browsing among the parts.

All the yardmen knew what the problem was, but nobody dared to say a word. At home Phyllis tried to take Seymour's mind off the shop, but on her own she went to Alonzo to see if she could make peace.

The black man lived on Willis Street in a gray two-story house that needed painting. His sister, Marie, who lived with him, taught second grade at the Willis Street School. Her three sons also lived in the house. Seymour used to brag about Alonzo's good family.

Johnson, a polite man in his early forties, welcomed Phyllis. Above his blue jeans and plaid shirt he wore a Muslim cap. In his living room was a photo of Elijah Mohammed and on the opposite wall a picture of an ancient Arab.

"You're welcome to my home," said Alonzo, "*Salam Alekham.*"

"I'm sorry," Phyllis said, "about the trouble between Seymour and you."

"So am I," the Muslim said.

"The baler is costing him a fortune in breakdowns."

"It's a shame," Alonzo said.

"Can't you go and tell him that you made a mistake?"

The black man looked at Phyllis. "A mistake?"

"Tell him it was a cult, they brainwashed you. You know Seymour wants you back. He'll believe it, he likes repentance."

"Mrs. Rubin," Alonzo said, "I told Seymour the truth as I see it. I can't change that."

"You really told him Hitler was right?"

"I told Seymour that he's a good man and I still think that even though he came at me with a sledgehammer."

"He hurt himself swinging at you."

"I didn't know until the next day. If I knew he was lying on the ground and hurt bad, I'd have come back. I got nothing against Seymour. Jews is another story."

"You're anti-Israel?' Phyllis asked.

"I am on the side of my oppressed Arab brothers."

"And you really told Seymour that Jews are scumbags?"

"I told him there were exceptions, and he was one."

"You know something?" Phyllis said. "I don't care what you think. I wish you'd go back and do your job. What you think is your own business."

"I agree," Alonzo said, "but Seymour owns the place. As usual, the Jew has got the power and the money."

Seymour was in the bathroom when Chuckie called. He knew that Phyllis had put their son up to it. Chuckie was no Alonzo, not yet, but a few weeks ago, when they discussed the Arab-Israel problems, from his own son Seymour Rubin heard these words: "Lay off the Jew stuff, will you, Dad? It's getting tiresome. I'm an American. The Indians are also my people."

Twenty-one years they'd been without children, and then the miracle. Chuckie, conceived when Seymour was forty-five and Phyllis forty-one, on the night that President Kennedy was assassinated, when they both lay in bed crying, and came together for comfort in their grief. Then their new life as older parents, with a healthy precocious boy, always the top of his class, curious, funny Chuckie, teasing his old bald father, calling him "Curly" at Fred's Barber Shop, where Seymour and his cronies, most of them bald, too, came in to have a trim and to talk sports.

Until he went to college Chuckie had all his haircuts at Fred's, too. Seymour liked to see Chuckie's red curls decorating the floor. For Chuckie alone Fred stacked a few comic books along with the sports and hunting magazines.

And then Chuckie went to college and everything changed. He stopped getting haircuts, he became a socialist, an anthropologist, a Ph.D. candidate. Seymour didn't even know what a Ph.D. was. And after Chuckie explained he still didn't know.

"Does this mean you'll be a philosopher with long hair and long fingernails?" Seymour asked.

Chuckie laughed. He still liked to tease Seymour about that one, though now he wasn't laughing or teasing, he was giving advice to his father.

"Dad," Chuckie said, when Seymour reluctantly came to the phone, "take Alonzo back. Whatever his opinions are, he's entitled to them. But more important, do what's good for you. You're not saving the Jewish people by losing your business and killing yourself. You don't have to go under to prove that you're right to a few crazy Black Muslims."

"Thank you for your opinion," Seymour said. "Now go back to your people the Indians."

When Chuckie's call did no good, Phyllis tried her own reasoning.

"Use your head," she said. "Hire him back and give the money he'll save you to Israel. That's the way a Jew can win."

That night Seymour was happy. He kissed Phyllis and called her

Henry Kissinger. But in the morning at his desk he couldn't dial the number. It might be smart to do so, but no cleverness could make Seymour work in the yard with a Hitler.

To save his business, Seymour thought of another plan, one that required help from Jews, not anti-Semites. He went to see the Lipson boys.

The boys were no longer boys, they were men in their mid-forties. Both Al and Larry had their father's big belly. Irv Lipson had been Seymour's competitor, but not cutthroat.

Right out of college his boys opened a do-it-yourself store on the land in front of his yard. They made a fortune on building supplies and already had two other warehouse stores. They let the old man handle the junk cars, but when he died, in 1986, they put in a huge shredder and began to buy auto scrap, not just from Muskegon but from all over lower Michigan. They leased a fleet of semis to handle the auto scrap and kept a ship docked at the port of Muskegon to send their shredded products straight to Japan.

Seymour had to call for an appointment—you couldn't just walk in on the boys. Now they were executives. In front of the salvage yard they had a domed building supply warehouse as big as a high school gym. Seymour could barely find a parking place.

The boys were friendly. They took Seymour into the yard to demonstrate their shredder. The Lipsons' machine didn't even sound like a baler.

Most of the cracking, Al explained, took place underground. The machine was as quiet as a truck in first gear.

"I've never seen a shredder before," Seymour admitted.

"Welcome to the twenty-first century, Seymour," Al Lipson said. "This is what's keeping the American scrap markets alive."

"What about breakdowns?" Seymour asked.

"No problem. Each part is replaced within two years. The factory does it on a regular schedule, on weekends for ten years. It's all part of the purchase price. You thinking of getting one, Seymour?

"No," he laughed, "I'm too old for this stuff."

"You're just like Dad," Al said, "he wouldn't let us touch the old baler while he was still alive."

After the tour the boys took Seymour into their office.

"What I'd like to do," he told them, "is sell you five hundred cars right away. I need some cash."

"We're not blind," Larry Lipson said, "we've noticed what's going on. But face it, Seymour, you're our competition. We've got a fortune tied up in the shredder, and because you still make the market in town we've got to lease trucks and run all over the state for cars to feed our shredder. We can't help you out. But if you're interested, maybe we can buy you out."

"Forget it," Seymour said. "When I'm dead you can talk to Phyllis and Chuckie."

"Seymour," Al Lipson said, "did you really come over thinking your competitors would help you?"

"Yes," said Seymour, "why not?"

"Because when it's tough for you it's good for us. That's business. You're nobody's fool, Seymour. You know that."

"What I know," Seymour said, "is that you're not starving, and I'm not starving. There's enough junk cars in Muskegon County for both of us to make a living."

"It's not about making a living," Al Lipson said. "It's not that simple these days. We carry an overhead you wouldn't believe. You don't just make a living anymore, you expand or collapse."

"Don't make me collapse."

"Seymour, be reasonable. Why should we prop you up?"

"Because you're Jews," Seymour said. "Because you owe that to another Jew."

The brothers looked at one another in surprise.

"Seymour," Al said, "this is not Poland a hundred years ago."

"You deny that you're Jews?" Seymour stood up.

"Of course not. We give to the UJA, we buy bonds, a lot more than you do. But what's religion got to do with this?"

"Everything," Seymour said. "I fired an anti-Semite, that's why I've got baler problems. When a fellow Jew comes to you for help you don't say no. This is what it means to be a people. I'm not a stranger to you."

Larry, who had been mostly silent, stood up behind his desk.

"Clever, Seymour," he said, "very clever, but it won't work. When you knew we had a shredder you raised your prices, you bought cars left and right. You didn't worry then about your cash flow and a clogged yard. Did we come to you and say how can you do this to Jews? Get off it, Seymour. And if you have come to sell, get this straight. We're only talking about raw land. In six more months your business will be history."

"Your father," Seymour said, "would turn in his grave if he heard you talking to me like this."

"People in graves don't turn," said Al Lipson. "It's that kind of thinking that's confusing you. Be realistic. Be smart, Seymour. Talk it over with Phyllis and Chuckie. Then come see us. Acre for acre you'll get a good price. You'll have enough to live out your life in Miami."

After barely sleeping, Seymour rose early on Saturday. He was not through with the Lipson brothers. Before services started, he was at Beth Jacob Synagogue, home of Muskegon's eighty-six-family Jewish community. On the cornerstone of the building was Seymour's name, along with Irving Lipson and two other Muskegon businessmen who had each contributed $10,000 to build the structure in 1955. Seymour at that time was still hitting motor blocks with a sledgehammer himself. That $10,000 he had earned with his own sweat, but he didn't say no to the community.

Now, every Saturday morning you could go to the synagogue to pray, though Seymour rarely did. The glass-enclosed bulletin board on Broadway listed Saturday services beginning at 9 am. Seymour was there waiting at 8:30. Nobody was in the building. The door was locked. Finally, at 9:45 Seymour saw Rabbi Hirsch drive up in an Oldsmobile. The car had a hole in the muffler. At any other time Seymour would have offered a muffler. Today he had other business.

In the sanctuary the rabbi apologized for being late.

"If anybody does come," he said, "it's not until 10 or 10:30. Last week, I was alone. Unless somebody gives a lunch afterward and makes sure his friends come, we never have a *minyan* on Saturday. Sometimes I'm here just to give tours and explanations to the gentiles."

"I'm not here to pray," Seymour said. He told the rabbi his business troubles, stressing to the clergyman the role of the Lipson brothers, whom he knew were prominent members of the congregation.

"I'm so sorry to hear this, Seymour," Rabbi Hirsch said. He touched Seymour's shoulder as if he'd learned that gesture in rabbinic school. "I know you've been sick. I visited you in the hospital as you recall. I remember that we had a nice conversation.

"What you tell me about the Muslims is not surprising. Unfortunately, I've read what's been going on in Chicago. It's only a few crazy people, but you're right to be alert to the dangers."

"The Muslim I took care of," Seymour said. "I need your help with the Lipsons. If they would shred a few hundred cars for me, my business wouldn't choke. It would take them one day, and I'd pay whatever they ask. Business is not war. You don't do this to anyone, especially not to a fellow Jew. This is what I hope you'll tell them."

The rabbi sat down in the empty synagogue.

"Seymour," he said, "I can't mingle in the private business of people in the community."

"What do you mean, you can't mingle? If you see something wrong, you can speak and give advice. You're the rabbi. People will listen."

"Seymour," Rabbi Hirsch said, "I wish everyone thought of rabbis as you do."

Rabbi Hirsch was a plump young man. He had two little daughters, and had come to Muskegon directly from the seminary. Like the previous rabbis, he would stay a few years, practice his sermon techniques, and then move to a better location.

"A rabbi can't tell a member how to run his private business."

"Then what can you do?"

Rabbi Hirsch, who had moved close, now slid back on the wooden pew.

"I can do pastoral counseling. I can help people through events in the life cycle. That's a rabbi's work."

"So if they squeeze me to death, you can say a *Kaddish* and deliver a nice eulogy, is that right?"

"It's not that stark, Seymour. The Lipson brothers, I'm sure, are ethical business people."

"I'm telling you they're not."

The rabbi walked to the bima. He put on a black polyester robe that covered his suit. Seymour, a congregation of one, now looked up at him. The rabbi spoke from the podium as if he was giving an official announcement.

"If the Lipson brothers were stealing or cheating, and if you had evidence, I would call them in. But business strategies are not a rabbinic area."

"If they were stealing," Seymour said, "I wouldn't come to you. I'd go to the police. I came here because a Jew doesn't squeeze another Jew. He recognizes something, brotherhood. Jews don't treat Jews as if they're strangers."

Eli Wolfson, a longtime member, had walked into the sanctuary. Standing at the rear door, he heard Seymour's words.

"Amen," he said. "Seymour, that's beautiful."

He tried to shake his old friend's hand, but Seymour didn't greet him as he ran from the synagogue.

In his car, Seymour felt as if he was choking. He had to stop on Monroe Avenue just to walk around and catch his breath. He stopped at a coffee shop to think things through. There, between breakfast and lunch, Seymour decided to swallow some principle, but not all. If his people turned him away, he was left with himself. But the business was not only himself. There were eleven employees. What would they do on Monday if Seymour didn't open? And Phyllis, what would her life be like if he sat home waiting for a call from the bankruptcy judge?

From the restaurant phone booth Seymour called the anti-Semite. Alonzo agreed to come to Seymour's house in an hour.

When the Black Muslim pulled up in his Mercury at a little past noon, Seymour greeted him dressed for the occasion. Deep in the closet, he found his tallis. It had yellowed with age and smelled like moth flakes. To go with it, Seymour placed a black skullcap over his thin gray hair. Let him see that he is dealing with a Jew, Seymour thought. He wanted to display an open Hebrew book, but he couldn't find one. Seymour invited the Muslim into the basement where they could have some privacy in case Phyllis returned from shopping.

Alonzo needed no explanation about the baler. "The brothers," he told Seymour, "keep me informed." Nor did the black man deny his desire to return, but he kept his conditions.

"Fridays noon to one, I teach in the baler room and I believe what I believe."

Seymour stayed calm. "It's a free country. I only want to know one thing. Why? What did Jews ever do to you? What did I ever do?"

"It ain't you, I said that all along."

"Without Jewish lawyers there wouldn't even be civil rights. You'd still be drinking from your own water fountains."

Alonzo was roaming the room. He examined Seymour's welded objects.

"Seymour," he said, "that's what all the white devils say. 'Without us you wouldn't have this and this and this. You'd still be jungle bunnies.' Well, if you white devils have been so good to us, how come we still got nothing?"

"What's this?" He held up a steel challah.

"That's Jewish bread," Seymour said, "for the Sabbath."

The black man glanced along the shelves. "All this is Jew stuff?"

"That's correct, Seymour said, "in my hobby I'm 100 percent Jewish."

The black man sat down opposite his former boss.

"So you ain't really one."

"One what?"

"A Jew. It's just a hobby?"

"No," Seymour said, almost laughing at Alonzo's misunderstanding. "I'm a Jew always, at home, at work."

"What you do with these?" The black man was holding in one hand a welded Torah, in the other a bagel.

Seymour was embarrassed that the scroll had such blunt and rough ends. The bagel, however, was good work, a nice clean circle.

"I don't do anything with them," Seymour said. "I make things and I put them on the shelf. It's a hobby, like stamp collecting. You know what a hobby is."

"Black people," Alonzo said, "got no time for hobbies."

"I didn't either," Seymour said, "but when Chuckie went away to college the house got so lonely. It still is."

"Your boy coming back?" Alonzo said, "I used to see him around the yard."

"No," Seymour said. "He wants no part of the yard, or Muskegon."

"He move to Israel?"

"No," Seymour said defensively. "He works with Indians on a reservation."

The black man stood. He offered Seymour his hand; reluctantly Seymour took it.

"Is Chuckie a Jew?" Alonzo asked.

Long after the black man left, Seymour, still in tallis and skullcap, sat in his workroom wondering.

Proton Decay

WHEN JEROME FELDMAN addressed himself to the woman lodged beneath three thousand tons of water he decided that he would not be coy. He would tell her at once that he was serious, yet he would do it in a way that wouldn't sound as if he was replying to a personal ad. After all, she had not advertised.

He had seen a feature on Irene Silver in the *Cleveland Plain Dealer* and then shortly thereafter saw her in person, or at least it seemed like that, on *60 Minutes*. The problem was, why would she be interested in him? And yet, why not? A single woman living underground for a month at a time—maybe a thriving pharmacist wouldn't sound so bad to her. Feldman, thinning hair, nearsighted, quiet in conversation but sure of himself, Feldman, at forty-six, sometimes felt hot.

Especially so on Thursdays after work, when he drove Grandma to the Imperial Salon. It was not unusual for a woman waiting for her stylist to prefer striking up a conversation with Feldman to browsing through a current magazine. Usually he was the only male in the waiting area, but he liked to take some credit beyond his gender. This month alone he had been given a business card by an attractive lawyer and by the regional representative of Sprint. He felt flattered by such attention, but he daydreamed only about Irene Silver.

While Grandma camped under the dryer, Feldman composed in his mind a letter to Ms. Silver. Jackie Norton, the Sprint representative, interrupted his reverie. "Nice to see you again," she said. She extended her hand and sat next to Feldman, only the width of her briefcase between them.

"I guess your grandmother and I have the same standing appointments," she said. Feldman smiled, stopped composing his letter so that he could concentrate on the slender, energetic woman so clearly flirting with him. "You didn't call," she said, and then she narrowed her eyes and made a child's sad face. She wiped away a feigned tear. "Just kidding, but I am disappointed."

"I've had a busy week," Feldman said.

"Workaholic?"

"Sometimes," he said.

"What did you tell me it was, drugstores?"

"Yes," he said, "and a package goods store. She runs it." He pointed toward the aquarium-sized hair dryer above Grandma's head. The manicurist noticed them and smiled in their direction. Feldman couldn't even see Grandma's face beneath the bowl of controlled heat, but her earrings, in the shape of Absolut vodka bottles, identified her.

"Is package goods liquor?" Feldman nodded. "And your grandma still works?" she asked.

"Yes," Feldman said. "She runs the store. There are four employees but she's the boss."

"That is amazing," Jackie said. She reached over to squeeze his hand. "I know you must help her a lot."

"Actually," Feldman said, "I just do the ordering. She's completely in charge."

When Grandma emerged from beneath the dryer, she tipped the stylist and the manicurist and walked toward Feldman. He introduced her to Jackie. Grandma barely noticed the woman. "Hello," she said. "Let's go. I want to brush out the stuff they put on me." Feldman held Grandma's elbow as she led him toward the door.

"Call me," Jackie said. Feldman waved, noncommittal.

His father had died when Feldman was twelve, and when his mother died she left him a drugstore, a liquor store, and Grandma. He had expected his grandmother to move to Florida, as her few remaining friends had. The old woman hadn't worked in a decade, but when she arose from mourning her daughter, she returned to the Grant Street liquor store. Feldman had been trying to sell the business for months, with no offers. Street people camped out in the doorway. The windows had been broken so many times that even after he installed steel bars he still couldn't get insurance. His most reliable employee, Philip, a serious young man from Liberia, had been shot at, and two other clerks had been robbed, though without assault. Before Grandma took over, Feldman himself hadn't dared to go near the store after dark. Still, he couldn't talk her out of returning to work, and legally, the store was still hers.

"I'd rather die quick in a robbery than die of boredom watching TV in that overheated apartment you got for me."

Grandma was eighty-nine when Feldman put the store which she and Grandpa had started back in her hands. With the help of Philip and the ironmonger who had installed the bars she built herself a tower in the center of the store, two ten-foot safety ladders, topped by a little booth the size of a parking-lot kiosk. From her lofty perch she could look straight at the security cameras and also scan the sales floor. Her eyesight, after cataract surgery, returned to 20–20, but she wore two hearing aids and still missed anything said in a conversational tone. At the store everyone yelled up to her. Feldman had expected her to last a week; she'd been there for three years without an incident. The men who came in to buy Ripple wine, the ones Feldman knew might've cut his throat for a bottle of cough syrup, threw kisses in the air to Grandma.

At ninety-two her health remained as stable as her profits. Whenever she needed to climb down, she buzzed for one of the floor clerks to assist her. For special customers she liked to toss down wall calendars or ballpoint pens, and every December, for the entire month, she dropped candy canes down to the customers who brought their children.

The regulars came to treat Grandma as a sage. Because of her years and her remoteness they thought of her as wise. Nobody was allowed to climb the stairs to see Grandma, but when she came down to eat or to go to the bathroom, there were people waiting to ask for advice about personal problems.

"I don't hear most of what they're talking about," she told Feldman. "But I say things like, 'You'll get over this. You'll get over everything.' It's the truth."

Feldman's own problems he didn't discuss with Grandma. He had expanded after his mother's death to a third location, the mall superstore where he did a high-volume business in cosmetics and small electronics and on certain items could almost match Wal-Mart. In the new store he watched himself become a wealthy man. He bought season tickets for his beloved Browns and Indians, but now that he had it, he wanted more than financial success. Women were available and Feldman had many times attempted to be in love. But, like Grandma, he told women the truth—he was waiting until he was sure.

At first he didn't take his interest in Irene Silver too seriously. He had an imagination. Sometimes he fantasized about a customer. Once while Feldman was trying to summon courage to speak to a woman who had caught his eye, he noticed her shoplifting shampoo and conditioner. He didn't even try to stop her—the price of his indulgence.

In the *60 Minutes* closeups the scientist looked composed, calm; and who could stay calm with Mike Wallace glaring at you? He liked the way she laughed, too, a big laugh when the interviewer asked her, "Don't you get lonely underground?"

"Of course," she said. And then she turned the tables on Wallace. "Don't you get lonely aboveground?"

Feldman, seated in front of his flat-screen TV, a slice of pizza in his hand, rose from his chair as if he'd just seen a sports highlight.

"Sometimes I'm lonely in the midst of company, too," the scientist said. "Loneliness doesn't have that much to do with being alone."

"Me, too," Feldman said to the television. "That's just how I feel." He continued to stand as the scientist, accompanied by the CBS crew, descended. At the bottom of the abandoned salt mine, Irene posed below an array of photomultipliers in her underwater laboratory.

"You're like a coal miner," Mike Wallace said.

"Not at all," the scientist answered. She wasn't falling for any of his lines. She held her lovely hand up to the camera. "No filth, no lung disease, no backbreaking work—I see no comparison to mining. I'm very fortunate to be able to do my work in such comfort and safety."

"And if you do find that a proton has decayed, do you think you'll win the Nobel Prize?"

Feldman thought she looked so beautiful, like a Christmas window display. The photomultipliers behind her appeared to be M&Ms glued to tinfoil. She ignored the camera as she glanced toward her instrument panel. "Prizes don't concern me," the scientist said. "First of all, I don't work alone. There are other depth locations in the United States and abroad. If we do confirm an event—greater certainty about the universe, that will be our prize."

"Yes!" Feldman yelled. At Ohio State he had taken three physics courses and felt a keen interest, but a drugstore always lay in his future so he leaned toward chemistry. When it came to matter, Feldman had penetrated no further than the outer electron shell.

"Certainty," he said aloud. "That's exactly what I want, too."

On Feldman Pharmacy stationery he began.

Dear Dr. Silver:

The idea of you beneath all that water is so moving. I am not a scientist but I admit to a lifelong interest in Dr. Albert Einstein. I have read the recent tome by Abraham Pais, which is a beautiful work even though Dr. Pais loses me whenever he switches from words to equations. Fortunately he realizes that many of us are not so adept at math so he makes it possible to skip the formulae and still get the life. I mean the essence of the work. What else is the life?

I am writing to you from my office at Feldman's Pharmacy in the Brady Oaks Mall; perhaps you have even been here? I read in the newspaper that when you come up, so to speak, for air, you like to shop in Cleveland. We have twenty-four thousand square feet of floor space and feature general merchandise as well as Cleveland's largest independent pharmacy.

Please do not think that I write to women all the time. You are the first and only. I am a serious man. May I suggest that we meet? In addition to the pleasure of seeing you face to face, I would like to talk about your work. If I understand correctly the decay of a single proton means that the entire universe will disintegrate. I look forward to discussing this with you.

Feldman looked up from his desk. It was 1 AM. Because it had an outdoor entry, the mall store stayed open all night. Like her work,

Feldman's also never ended. But the certainties he pursued were far more modest. He had the routine of commerce, the steady revolution of seasonal goods, the holiday markdowns, the readjustments of Medicare reimbursement. Feldman, in good health and with his revenue growing at 20 percent year over year, came to the conclusion that he had little chance with the scientist. Irene Silver looked toward the end of time; at 8:30 every morning Feldman took Grandma to Dunkin' Donuts and then on to Grant Street. He reread his letter, then he crumpled it.

An only child of an only child, Feldman had always been Grandma's boy, her little helper. When Grandma heaved in her foaming bath there stood five-year-old Feldman, lifeguard on the other side of the shower curtain. His mother and Grandma would take their little pharmacist-to-be into ladies' rooms with them, into the tiny curtained dressing rooms at Simpson's Department Store, where skirts fell like spilled drinks and price tags dangled at their arms. At a young age he observed females up close, knew the underarm pad and the hook-and-eye snap. He loved the company of women and yet he had passed up marriage opportunities, satisfied with the occasional cashier or cosmetics clerk while he built his business.

Work was what Feldman knew. In grade school he had straightened aspirin bottles and dusted shelves. In high school he organized the stockroom and in college he took phone orders and alphabetized prescriptions

Both his parents worked until the day of their death and that was Grandma's plan, too. These were his models. When he put off marriage, he assumed that his own life would swell on like Grandma's, but who could know? With a station wagon full of greeting card returns his father, only fifty, had slumped at the wheel forever. The word reminded him of Irene Silver. What did time mean to someone who awaited an event, that if it happened at all, might take seven billion years?

A few days after his attempted letter and even before Grandma's next hair appointment, Jackie Norton called to announce that she was in his very mall. Feldman walked to the Circuit City store to see her, then invited her to Ming's for lunch. The sales representative ate her salad daintily and with chopsticks. Feldman admired her skill. As she chewed, she explained the secrets of cell phone miniaturization. "I'm having my hair done on Thursday as you know, and it will still look good on Saturday."

The following Saturday night in the more romantic atmosphere of Brands Steakhouse, after a bottle of wine and much smiling and nodding of her head, Jackie got down to business. She reached into her purse and then placed her delicate closed fists on the table in front of Feldman.

"Curious?" she asked. She turned her fists in the candlelight as if she was trying to sell him her watch. Feldman admitted his curiosity. "Go ahead," Jackie said. She held her closed hands toward him.

Feldman hesitated, not sure whether to open finger by finger or, in the more manly fashion, all four at once. He decided one by one, starting with her red-tipped pinky. In the middle of her palm, an offering—wrapped in black foil, decorated with the image of a Greek warrior—a condom.

"I'm in communications," Jackie said, "and there's nothing more important to communicate about these days, is there?"

Feldman, accustomed to seeing cases at a time, looked with surprise at one.

"We're adults," Jackie said. "There's lunch, there's dinner, there's this."

She said it slowly, drawing out each word the way the announcer at the ballpark listed the Indians batting order: leading off, "lunch"; batting second, "dinner." Batting a third, "this." She paused for a minute. "Carl, my ex, he refused to use them. But that was the least of his flaws. I hope you're not against safe sex."

Feldman shook his head. "I'm all for it." He wanted to feel something like lust, some reason to close his hand around hers and say, "Let's go—right now." Jackie Norton looked so lovely, too, her bosom accommodating, her cheeks rosy—though it might have been makeup. But instead of imagining her panting beneath him Feldman pictured his own condoms in their revolving rack at the end of aisle 12.

"I hope you don't think I'm too aggressive," Jackie said. She kept her hand over the object. "I've learned in sales that you don't help yourself if you save your best for later. Sometimes there's no later."

Feldman nodded. "You're absolutely right," he said. And then, he surprised himself. "I'm flattered," he said, "and most of the time I would be . . . You know . . . Right with you. But at this time, I'm taken." Jackie didn't try to disguise her feelings. Feldman looked away, giving her the privacy of shame. In her disappointment, he felt genuine tenderness toward Jackie, though he decided not to hug,

"I wish you had told me right away," she said.

"I should have," he admitted. "I'm sorry."

"Well, she's a lucky woman to have such an honest guy."

Jerome Feldman, the outgoing president of the Ohio Association of Independent Pharmacists, decided that he would be assertive and honest. Like his fellow independents he worried about Rite Aid and Walgreens and looked forward to seeing colleagues on a yearly basis. The annual convention keynote speaker alternated between extremes, one year an Ohio legislator, the next year a comic entertainer.

"I know that this is our year for scheduling a comedian," Feldman announced to the board. "But I have taken the liberty of inviting a scientist to speak to us." Feldman looked out at the fourteen pharmacists on the board. Not a hand went up in objection.

"A real scientist," he went on even though he didn't have to. "Someone who's doing pure research."

Connie, Feldman's secretary, made the call. Dr. Silver was surprised and delighted. She was not accustomed to trade association invitations. She said it would be no trouble for her to come to Cleveland on whatever day the group wanted her. Her schedule was very flexible.

"When I told her that we pay a thousand dollars, she didn't believe me," Connie said. "She goes, 'For one speech?' That's the going rate, I told her. She should hear the comedy people complain that it's not enough. She sounds nice but she didn't seem too sure about what we want her to talk about. Maybe you should give her a call."

This opportunity, too, Feldman declined. Not with her would his first exchange take place over such long and imprecise wavelengths. On the phone nothing was true enough. On the phone Grandma could chirp like a teenager. On the phone Einstein once told an interviewer, "Idea? I've never had an idea." When the time came for him to speak to Irene Silver, he would tell her both his position and his velocity.

A few days after she had accepted the invitation, Dr. Silver mailed in her credentials, her facts, etched in 12-point type. She had no middle name, no husband, no children. Feldman already knew this from Google. She was thirty-eight, hobbyless as well. She had gone to Cornell and Harvard. Her work she labeled merely "a study of proton decay."

Feldman loved her modesty. No fancy language, no mention of the foundations and universities that had supported her research. Just a plain Jane of neutrino physics. Her accompanying letter was clear and direct, addressed to Connie—who else did she know?

Dear Connie Denison:

Thank you and your committee for inviting me to speak. I will be happy to do so on August eleventh.

Feldman kept the folded letter in his pocket, memorized the résumé, and waited for August eleventh.

During the heat wave in the month of July, Feldman's stores boomed. He ran out of Sunblock and then Afterburn and Unguentine. Grandma reordered wine coolers twice a day. The superstore sold in a month the season's supply of chaise lounges and barbecue grills and electric fans. Feldman, looking at sales printouts, could hardly believe how far he had come from the days when his father would carry home the receipts in a small briefcase. Yet, he did not want to introduce himself to Dr. Silver as a businessman. He wanted to sound more romantic and then, as he thought of romance, Feldman's heart clogged with jealousy. He began to imagine his competitors. After all, he had no idea with whom she stayed underground. Harvard men, pipe smokers, precise thinkers, men as patient and intelligent as Dr. Silver herself, men who would laugh if she told them that she had begun seeing a pharmacist in Cleveland. Feldman, on bad days, calculated his chances: one in ten? in a hundred? a thousand? On people who lived underground there were no statistics. The jealousy tortured him but he also enjoyed it. She was keeping him on his toes.

As the date of her speech approached, he thought about her more and more. He gave her personal idiosyncrasies. To her professional résumé he added a biography. She disliked animals, had a small streak of physical vanity. She was always polite but sometimes distant, like the women in perfume ads. But when she wanted to speak, to be warm, friendly, interested, boy oh boy could she do it.

By early August Feldman hardly paid attention to daily life. Grandma called twice about a late shipment of Mohawk brandy, then she sent Philip to check on him. The Liberian walked all the way from Grant Street, entered winded and sweating. "You okay, Mr. Boss?" Philip asked. "Grandma, she's worried about you."

Feldman offered a 16-oz. Coke. "I'm okay. It's just business, I'm too busy."

After downing the cola, the African cleared his throat. "I'll be leaving—around Thanksgiving, going back to Liberia."

"Going back? After all the war and the killing that you witnessed?"

"It's not that way any more," Phillip said. "There's no more gangs, and the president is educated—a woman. I'm thinking of maybe going into politics myself."

Though stunned, Feldman admired the man's courage and knew it would not be easy to replace him, but how could he compare a new hire with a new life. "I really think it's wonderful, and I want to help." While Philip waited near an air-conditioning vent Feldman went to his office to write a huge bonus check, half a year's salary.

Feldman hated horoscopes and long ago had dispatched God to the clearance bin, but he took Philip's decision as a good omen for all risk-takers. On August tenth he prayed that Irene Silver would take a chance, too, that she would see him as he was and be satisfied.

Before she walked up to the podium Feldman observed her from a distance. Anonymous among the group of pharmacists snacking on hors d'oeuvres, he would wait until she finished her speech to make his own. He watched as she peeled a celery stalk as if it was a banana, making a small meal of the celery and a few baby carrots. It pleased Feldman to notice that she, too, seemed a little nervous. She scanned the room looking, he knew, for him.

Three days before her appearance, Feldman finally e-mailed his feelings, not all but enough. Irene Silver wrote back telling him that his words made her blush. He had attached a photo as well and instead of a résumé, he ordered flowers delivered to her deep underground. One of them, a fading orchid, perched, as she spoke, between her heart and her left shoulder. Feldman told her where he would be sitting, described his suit and his tie. Five rows back, he placed himself where her eyes could alight comfortably on him and they did.

Dr. Silver spoke to the assembled pharmacists about the neutrino, the almost massless particle. With its nonzero weight and without charge it sailed through the cosmos equally indifferent to all matter. Every second a few billion neutrinos passed through Cleveland on their way . . . the scientist paused. "I can't say where they are going; nothing will stop them so the journey is endless."

As she spoke people coughed and buttoned their clothes against the frigid air conditioning. Some politely tiptoed toward the exits. Feldman, riveted, knew that she spoke directly to him.

"Why doesn't she say anything about drugs?" a man on his right whispered. "I wish she'd talk about baldness or Alzheimer's. Who gives a shit about neutrinos?"

When Irene Silver finished to scattered applause, from the back of the auditorium Feldman heard the shriek of Grandma's hearing aids. He had brought Grandma, too. There would be no secrets kept from Irene Silver. Feldman wanted to present her with everything: the three stores, his dead parents, the accumulated experience of his life as a man.

He rose to introduce himself to the woman he had chosen to love. She watched him approach and held out her hand. "I hope you're not disappointed," she said.

Feldman, too overcome to speak, took her hand and held it. He was thinking about Liberia for a honeymoon, but first, he understood, the lady would need some time to decide about the universe.

Stabbing an Elephant

WHEN MR. JACOBSON took off his snowy overcoat and told me "we" had a problem, I thought he spoke of the marital we.

"Should I speak to Mrs. Jacobson as well?" I asked.

"No," he said, "my wife and I are in complete agreement. This is the problem, Rabbi."

He handed me a thin blue booklet, "The Story of Hanukkah," written and illustrated by Zvi Herman. "Look at page 6," he ordered.

I saw a colorful illustration—an ancient soldier wearing leather headgear and sandals jabbed his short sword into an elephant's belly. Although the elephant's knees buckled, the animal seemed otherwise undisturbed. The soldier looked up at the beast as casually as a mechanic examines a Buick on the rack.

"This is giving my child nightmares," Mr. Jacobson said. "Should a four-year-old be exposed to this, especially in a religious school environment?"

"War is awful," I agreed, "the children understand that Eleazar, Judah Maccabee's brother, is a hero defending his people and his faith."

"Rabbi," Mr. Jacobson said, "I'm talking about the elephant, not the man."

"But the story is about the man, the elephant is just a tank in a war story."

"You don't have to explain that to me—I'm talking about a four-year-old, a four-year-old who loves elephants and is inconsolable."

"I'm sorry," I said, "I had no idea. This seems so tame compared to cartoons."

"Beth doesn't watch cartoons," Mr. Jacobson said. "She sleeps with Babar in one hand and his wife, Celeste, in the other. After her fourth birthday she asked us to send all her presents to an African game reserve for the elephants."

"A remarkable child," I said.

"She is," Mr. Jacobson said. "As you can see I married late in life. What I'm learning from her . . . it chokes me up, Rabbi . . . this child is so precious to me."

"Of course," I said, "I feel terrible about this. If it's okay with you, I'll come to your home tonight to speak with Beth."

"What will you tell her?"

"Maybe we'll talk about the candles rather than the war."

Mr. Jacobson shook his head. "Not tonight, we're having a consultation with Bill Hazelton, the head of psychiatry at the med school. You may know that Helen, my wife, is a psychotherapist. She told Bill what's been going on and he's seeing Beth tonight as a professional favor. I don't think Beth needs a psychiatrist and a rabbi in one evening."

I agreed.

"But it's an important matter," he said. "In the last two days Beth has regressed six months."

"Does that put her back to Passover?" I quipped.

"It puts her back to diapers," Mr. Jacobson said. "This is not a joking matter. Beth is at a crucial developmental stage. Her value system is under attack. She's been taught that the Jewish soldiers are good and she knows without teaching that elephants are good. Can you understand the dilemma?

"I'll call you in the morning, Rabbi," he said, "to discuss Dr. Hazelton's recommendations."

This was the biggest crisis of my brief career as a rabbi. Harold Solomon, my immediate predecessor at Temple Emanuel, now had a small congregation in Atlanta. In spite of rumors about him and several married women, he was enormously popular. After six years he grew weary of waiting for Rabbi Edwards to retire.

I benefited from his impatience. In this, only my second year, Rabbi

Edwards announced his retirement. He did so from the pulpit on Rosh Hashanah.

"Beginning next Friday evening," he said—then he paused. He was the master of the dramatic pause. This time he surprised the entire congregation. "Next Friday evening and thereafter . . . I am going to share the pulpit on a biweekly basis with my distinguished junior colleague, Rabbi Wohlman."

Everyone knew what that meant. He had selected me to succeed him. Rabbi Solomon's fans, mostly the young marrieds and the singles, were not happy.

They plotted. The board held a meeting, but my supporters prevailed. Dr. Firestone, an orthopedic surgeon, the current president, met with me.

"You know that Rabbi Solomon had great rapport with much of the congregation. Every summer he led a young couples' adventure tour."

"I've heard him praised," I said.

"I told his fans," Dr. Firestone said, "that we needed a rabbi, not a tour guide, but you might think about taking a group somewhere. The only criticism I heard was that you're not as adventurous as Rabbi Solomon."

"There were no classes in adventure at the seminary," I said.

Dr. Firestone smiled. "That's a relief," he said, "but you know what I'm getting at, people liked Harold because they say he didn't act like a rabbi—I'm just passing that on for what it's worth."

"I'll keep it in mind," I said, and I did; only I wasn't sure how not to act. Adventure seemed easier. I contacted a travel agency that specialized in it. I could lead a prayer service in the Amazon, along the Urubumba River, or while ballooning in New Zealand, each at about the same price. I chose the Amazon thinking it would be a relief from snowy Detroit. Thus far, no congregants had reserved a space, but there was still plenty of time.

In the morning just before Mr. Jacobson called, Jane Kaplan, a young divorcée who had gone on Rabbi Solomon's Urubumba trip, stopped to criticize my selection.

"We've been to South America," she said. "Why not try another continent?"

Her blue body stocking indicated that she was either coming from or going to aerobic dancing. Even in my office she twitched. There had been rumors about her and Rabbi Solomon, but I tried to drive slander from my thoughts.

"Not everyone has been there," I said, "but I'm glad you're giving me feedback. You're the first to respond."

She looked around my small office as if she might find something on the walls beyond my degrees and photos of my brother's children.

"There used to be a photograph of Harold and the entire group in rubber suits. It was hilarious."

From the look in her eyes I knew that no matter what trip I might propose, I would never be her rabbi.

She was still in the room when Mr. Jacobson called to say that Dr. Hazelton thought a retraction would be necessary.

"Retract what?" I asked.

"The elephant," he said. "Tell the children that this event never happened, that the illustration was a mistake."

For what happened next I have no good explanation, only a theory. Until this point, Mr. Jacobson and I had not been having a dispute. I had no vested interest in the Book of the Maccabees, One or Two, and I certainly wanted to make Beth feel better. But the word *retract* stung me. Maybe it was his imperial manner or the challenge to my authority—whatever. No doubt, Jane Kaplan, standing at the doorway listening, didn't help. All this roused what the rabbis called the *Yetzer Hara*, loosely translated as "evil impulse."

"No," I told him, "I can't change the story. The elephant is a recorded fact; it's history. I can't interpret it away."

Mr. Jacobson reacted as if I had lashed him with a whip.

"I've told you how much this means to my child—how much she and her mother and I are in distress over this and you refuse to make a simple retraction?"

"I have no authority to do so," I said.

"We'll see," Mr. Jacobson said.

When Dr. Firestone got in touch with me a few hours later, I forgot about Hanukkah. The specific charge was child abuse.

"Believe me, I hate to tell you this," Dr. Firestone said.

"I never touched the child. You know that, Mr. Jacobson knows it, Beth knows it."

"Of course you didn't. It's a legal term. Jacobson is a lawyer—he used a legal term. I'm sorry, but I had no choice. I called for an emergency board meeting tonight at 7:30. We want you to have a chance to tell your side of the story."

I went immediately to Rabbi Edwards's study.

"You want my advice?"

"Of course," I said.

Rabbi Edwards had a full head of silver hair and enunciated every syllable.

"Cut the elephant; it's apocrypha, not Torah."

"It doesn't seem right," I said. "It's the one detail that always made the story seem real to me."

"Who's gonna care?" Rabbi Edwards asked, "ten four-year-olds? Look, I've known Sy Jacobson for twenty-five years. Sure he's a little nuts about his kid. He was a bachelor until he was forty-eight. I can't tell you how many times women called me to ask about him when he was president of the temple. I told them all, 'I'm a rabbi, not a marriage broker.' I thought he was gay myself. Then one day he called, told me he was in love and that was it. They got married right here in the study."

"So you would do it because he's your friend?"

"I would do it," Rabbi Edwards said, "because you're running a nursery school, not the Sanhedrin. If you're going to succeed with this or any congregation you'll have to learn to take your stand on things that matter, otherwise you'll throw away all the good will you have. Good will, that's a rabbi's capital. Waste it and it's gone forever."

"Will you be at the board meeting?" I asked.

He shook his head. "I'll be in Orlando for the Interfaith Council meeting. I'm leaving in an hour." He put an experienced hand on my shoulder. "God tests us all," he said, "but this, this isn't from God, it's from *Sesame Street*. Settle it quickly."

I knew, as I walked along the deserted school corridor, that I had two clear choices. I could retract the elephant or, like Judah Maccabee's brother, let it crush me.

From the window of my school office I saw a Yellow Cab come for Rabbi Edwards. I watched Detroit darken and my Honda Accord begin to disappear beneath soft thick snow. The secretary saying good-bye startled me at five. Alone in the empty building, I opened Maccabees One. The elephant was there. I could almost see him—not Babar, but a big gray tusk-heavy bull bearing down on the Jewish people. I watched the battle unfold as if it was an adventure movie. Judah and his brothers had seen the temple desecrated, the pious destroyed, and in a line that startled me, I read that even the beauty of the Hebrew women had been altered.

Not one elephant, but thirty-two marched against the Maccabees, and Eleazar, the elephant slayer, did not resemble his warrior brother. Perhaps because of the illustration in Beth's book, I imagined him thin, sandals and headgear a size too large.

The elephants had been fed grape and mulberry juice to enrage them. On its back, in bucket seats, each beast carried four powerful men. The noise of this army marching from Antioch clogged Eleazar's ears. The sun bouncing from their brass shields lighted the mountains. He choked on the dust—his comrades who had fought for a generation fled before these machines of destruction, and then, this modest man, this overlooked brother—something happened to him. He stepped forward, out of himself into history. Far be it from me to remove him.

When I closed the book it was 7:20 and my heart was pounding. With two fingers, on the typewriter Rabbi Solomon had left behind, I wrote my letter of resignation. I had just finished when Beth's preschool teacher, Julie, knocked and then entered. I had instructed Julie last year in conversion class and had been seeing her socially, less regularly than she wished, but I told her that I wanted to solidify my career before making larger plans.

"Why are you doing this?" she asked. "Why are you throwing away your career over an elephant?"

At that moment, fired by the story, I felt heroic myself—also strongly attracted to Julie. Her concern showed. Like the women in the text her beauty had been altered by struggle, to me heightened. I wanted to embrace her, but in the hallway I heard the eight board members.

"I appreciate your concern," I said. "I'm trying to do what a rabbi should do."

"I don't understand you," she said, "to give the jerks what they want you're willing to take a tour group to the Amazon, but to keep a sweet little girl from having nightmares you won't retract an elephant."

"I can't," I said. "The elephant is history, the jerks aren't."

"You know they'll fire you, don't you? Sy Jacobson has the board in his pocket. He's a past president and an important lawyer and his wife is on TV all the time. You can't fight them."

"I'm not fighting anybody," I said. "I'm making a rabbinical decision."

Ten minutes later I said the same thing to the board. Julie was in the room with the eight temple trustees, so was Mr. Jacobson. As if in court, I sat across the room from my accuser. In the hallway Beth, clutching Babar dressed in a green vest, waited with her Latin American babysitter.

"First," I said, "I regret whatever anxiety I have brought to Beth. This concerns me more than anything else. But if I set a precedent here, what will I tell a parent whose child loves rams when he or she comes to me next September demanding the ram be omitted from the story of the sacrifice of Isaac? To please that child, should I let Abraham kill his son?"

"We're talking about an elephant, not a ram," Mr. Jacobson said. "We're talking about a specific child, not a theoretical one. Don't confuse the issue."

"May I invite Beth in?" I asked Mr. Jacobson.

"Yes," he said. "She wants to be here—to see justice done."

I faced the lawyer, the teacher, and the child. I had King Solomon's example before me, also Rabbi Solomon's. King Solomon would have ferreted out the true solution; Rabbi Solomon would have taken the child to an elephant love-in in Thailand. I had neither the wisdom of old Solomon nor the adventurous spirit of young Solomon. I had a sweet child before me, a father who would turn the world upside down for her, and a teacher who understood elephants, but not rabbis.

"I want to correct one thing in the Book," I told Beth. "What really happened was slightly different. In those days people usually rode on camels. The soldier killed a camel, not an elephant, and he was very sad about that, but he had to do it."

Mr. Jacobson gave me a suspicious look, then waited for Beth. Dr. Firestone and the board both waited. Julie waited. Beth, in a strong voice, decided.

"You can't change an elephant to a camel." She moved onto her father's lap.

Jacobson smiled, proud of his daughter's cleverness. I handed my letter of resignation to Dr. Firestone.

Julie crouched on her knees—eye level to the child.

"Beth," she said, "you know I wasn't born Jewish. I changed. And how do you think that happened?"

Beth shook her head; she didn't seem to care.

"I had to really want to do it, and it wasn't easy," Julie said. "If people can change, why can't elephants?"

Beth hesitated, considering the possibility. She looked at me and I saw beneath her trimmed bangs eyes that had studied species variation in *Where the Wild Things Are.*

She shifted her weight, causing her father's swivel chair to move as she looked at him for advice.

Mr. Jacobson said nothing. Julie, still crouching beside Beth, made the case silently for the camel and all other converts.

"Are you going to change again?" Beth asked her teacher.

"I can answer that," I said. "Julie's not going to change, but I am."

Before the child made up her mind, I did. In front of the assembled board, I took my first adventure trip—across the room to Julie.

"I guess it's okay," Beth said, in a quiet voice that I hardly heard.

I reached for Julie's hand, but her pupil, quickened by relief, jumped from her father's lap and beat me to it.

Peace

On the fourth of July, Jay Wilson and his partner, Leo, always threw a big party. They gave away four or five cases of pellet snakes, a gross of sparklers, paper American flags, Uncle Sam masks, just about everything that was on page 5 of their catalogue. But this year they were short of goods, and Leo wouldn't stop blaming the Koreans.

"They discovered cars and electricity," Leo told the guests, "and then they forgot about loyalty. They forgot about contracts and about people like us who taught them everything." While Leo complained about the Orientals, Jay kept quiet and knew this would be his last Fourth of July in Florida.

The Korean suppliers were making things hard, but Jay didn't blame them. Gifts and novelties were not high-profit items. Jay was the one who had gone to Seoul fresh out of Florida State and come out with two million charcoal pellets that turned into snakes as they burned. He'd paid three cents apiece in Korea and sold the whole lot in the United States for seventeen cents apiece, in Canada for twenty.

The snakes were the boost that made the two fraternity brothers entrepreneurs in the mail-order business. Leo liked to brag about it. "We're not into clothes," he'd say. "Otherwise, L. L. Bean would be shaking in their rubber boots."

Jay knew better. He credited their modest success to timing. They went into business in 1978, during the golden age of mail order. People were still worried about gasoline shortages and inflation. They liked to look at photos and use their new credit cards. Before Jay and Leo had a real office, while they were still undergraduates, they had an 800 number. In their senior year of college, they both made decent grades and a twenty-thousand-dollar profit. After graduation they took their catalogue business national.

But the partners never saw eye to eye. Jay liked the trinkets they sold, Leo thought they were all junk. Leo put his earnings into a Corvette, a condo, and a twenty-four-foot motorboat. He was clearing about forty thousand dollars a year and thought he was Rockefeller because they had a nineteen-page catalogue and money came every day in the mail.

Lately, Leo complained all the time. The Hong Kong and Taiwan suppliers were late with the improved pocket rain-bonnets and the flat Frisbees; and as for the Koreans, J & L Inc. hadn't seen a charcoal snake in six months. The Koreans weren't even answering Leo's faxes.

"You oughta get your ass over to Manila or Pakistan," Leo said, "find us some suppliers we can trust to deliver."

"Why don't you go?" Jay said.

"You think you're a hotshot, don't you? You got to rub it in, like you're my enemy."

Leo would never leave the United States. He preferred not to leave Tallahassee. Even Miami was too foreign for him. "I know the rest of the world is not out to get me," Leo said, "and I'm not gonna bother them either. I've got everything I want right here."

On the inside front cover the J & L catalogue said: "We searched the world for bargains," but after Jay's trip to Korea, they searched the world by searching other catalogues and talking to other distributors. Almost every season new opportunities came their way. Most of them they ignored. Jay let Leo's conservatism influence him. Together they decided not to distribute the Hacky Sack, and they turned down the banana purse and the inflatable greeting card.

Leo was happy enough with his Corvette and his boat. He wanted his life to be like a beer commercial, only in slow motion.

But Jay, now past thirty, wanted out of Tallahassee—and not to the Third World. He wanted to live in New York.

"That would be great," Leo said, "if we were shipping Jewish lawyers by the case."

When J & L celebrated its tenth anniversary, Jay lit his last company sparkler.

"You're nuts," Leo said, "you're walking out of paradise to go live with rats."

Still, Leo was happy to mortgage his house and his boat in order to buy Jay out. He agreed to pay 5 percent of net for the next twenty years as goodwill. Unless Leo got himself another partner, Jay suspected that there would never be a next twenty years. Leo would go under selling military insignias and rubber beer-can holders. Right from the start the business had been all Jay's. Leo was a partner because in college he had a car and could make deliveries.

Jay actually had wanted to move to New York right after college, but he and Leo had those two million snake pellets and then there were the six-foot feather dusters and the American flags with collapsible poles—every year another project to keep him in Tallahassee talking on the phone, turning the pages of the J & L book. It was a good living, but not the life he wanted.

Abraham Huang, in New York, understood this. For more than a year Jay and Huang had been penpals. Jay wrote Huang a letter after reading a small item about him in *Business Week*. The magazine called him "Mr. Cube." Huang did not invent the Rubik's Cube, but he merchandised it brilliantly. He bought 3.5 million units wholesale and sat on them. Then the craze broke out. Six months later, just before the imitators came in and drove the price down to ninety-nine cents, Huang sold out. He was now a consultant in New York who charged a thousand dollars a day for his advice.

In a letter to Mr. Cube, Jay flattered the entrepreneur's foresight and described his own career.

Huang wrote back. "Many envy well. But you are first to admire product decision. Thank you, Mr. Fan." Jay wrote back to the millionaire, and after that, about once a month, they exchanged first-class mail.

Abraham Huang did not have an office or a driver's license or a computer. He explained to Jay that his cousin, James Huang, drove him through New York in a 1985 Dodge. "As I ride, I get ideas. Not exactly ideas, thoughts about how to act. When I sit in office, I feel stale. In car, if I am not thinking, I look out window— like seeing a movie."

When Jay wrote to tell Huang that he was thinking of cashing in his Florida business and taking the plunge in the Big Apple, Abraham Huang sent a one-word letter. "Come."

But once Jay was in New York, the consultant, though friendly and cheerful, kept his distance. He did invite him to sit in the backseat of his Dodge on a sightseeing tour. But as they cruised through the city, Huang read the Chinese newspaper and his cousin James mentioned places in English so imperfect that Jay, after James's first four thank yous, didn't try to respond. He sat in the backseat and read the street signs. When James pulled up in front of Jay's apartment building, Huang put down his newspaper.

"This time West Side. Next time East Side," he said.

"Listen," Jay said, "I really appreciate the tour. But you guys don't have to bother. I've got a good map and for sightseeing I can take one of those boat tours."

"East Side very interesting," Huang said. He then spoke Chinese to James, who quickly got out of the car to shake hands with Jay.

"Make good fortune in New York," James said. He moved his hand through the air like a jet plane. "East Side we go."

After his West Side tour, Jay stayed close to home. He made it his job to learn his neighborhood, Broadway between 110th and 125th. That much seemed manageable. Every morning after reading the *Times* he walked through his territory, seeing the sights and handing out quarters. At Grant's Tomb he turned around and headed back downtown.

In New York everything was for sale. He bought a rug from a man who wore a gold chain bearing the letters *G-O-D*. Jay was trying to get away from him, but at 113th Street the salesman, running alongside to keep up with Jay's long strides, spread the carpet over the curb. On the rug an Arabian woman emerged from a lamp. Serpents coiled around her arms. Remembering his Korean snake pellets, Jay considered the design a good omen. He paid fifty dollars and spread the rug beside his bed.

This kind of direct merchandising appealed to him. The blood and bones of New York—the business of real estate—was to Jay Wilson as remote as the moons of Jupiter. When he looked at a building all he saw was a place to live. For profit he liked a product, preferably something pocket-size, lightweight, and under five dollars.

He told Abraham Huang when they had coffee one afternoon on Canal Street that he felt camaraderie with the Indians who sold Manhattan for beads. Huang put down his cup and shook the younger man's hand.

"You know value," he said. "Now we go see."

James drove them to the warehouses, first near the docks, then deep into the Lower East Side. On Rivington Street, where they looked at cartons of stretchable watchbands and ladies' vinyl pumps, the consultant spoke openly to Jay.

"This," Huang said, pointing from the boxes they surveyed toward the Hudson River, "this is true. In big world all million dollars. Wall Street, Saks Fifth Avenue, Hotel Plaza. Here, underworld. Twenty-five cent, maybe $2.99, maybe $3.49. Real numbers."

Jay listened and felt like a brother. Together they stuck their fingers into drums of bottle openers and toothpaste rollers. They held up delicate paper fans and admired flower-shaped ice-cube trays, bath cushions in the shape of a woman's lips, squeezable change purses.

Abraham Huang took him to six or seven locations. They rode in dingy freight elevators and looked at goods under bare bulbs. Not even in Korea had Jay seen such variety. Huang paused in sorrow over a crate of purple handbags.

"Stale color," he said, "impossible." Then he reached into a bin and pulled out several ballpoint pens. "Jane's Bar, Albuquerque," he read, "665–2380." Then, "Ted's Texaco, Ishpeming, AAA Roadwork." He put the pens into his pocket.

"Molded plastic," Abraham Huang said, " always good to read."

At dusk, on the third floor above a Grand Street lamp factory, Jay Wilson stopped to consider an open crate of swords. The jobber stood beside him.

"This is all that's left of *Star Wars*," the man said.

Jay recognized the *Star Wars* sword. It had been a big hit in the toy stores. He pulled out a two-foot weapon with a red handle. The sword was rounded, more a wand than a blade. He pulled it through the air to listen to its distinctive whoosh. Abraham Huang moved back as if in fear.

"Eight years ago," the jobber said, "it was $7.95, if you could find it. At Toys "R" Us they were getting full price even after Christmas. This sword has never been discounted. It got old before its time. When the new shipments came in, the toy stores had already rolled their inventory twice and gone on to Indiana Jones.

"You may think *Star Wars* is dead," the jobber continued, "but eight million times a year those movies rent out. Hardly a day goes by that you don't hear a kid charging someone with a stick and yelling that The Force is with him. And now for ten cents apiece—the price of the packaging—whoever buys this becomes the Pentagon of *Star Wars*. You'll get every one there is."

The jobber kicked the crate. Jay looked at Abraham Huang. Mr. Cube smiled.

Jay took the jobber's card. The swords twinkled like silver dollars, but Jay, a cautious man, wanted to think things over. At a dime a crack, he was getting a major item, about this there was no doubt. In his catalogue days he had paid more than a dime for Abraham Lincoln thimbles and candle-drip collectors. The sword was not a dimer. It was a two-foot bicolor piece and it even made a sound. Like the Hula-Hoop with a stone inside, it was something unique. Still, it was dead and might stay dead forever. Jay thought of the purple vinyl handbags, a dead item he would never touch. Then he decided that the sword was sellable, the problem was quantity. He didn't want all 600,000. In the morning he telephoned the jobber.

"No dice," the wholesaler said. "I thought Huang told you: No split lots. For chicken feed I'm not going to deliver twice. This one is either all or nothing."

That afternoon, to test himself, Jay called Leo. His former partner snorted into the phone.

"Buy 'em," he said, "then stab yourself 600,000 times."

Leo was predictable; but Jay wasn't going to make a business decision just to spite Leo. The stakes were too high. He had to think this one through. The sword would never again see $7.95, but he could buy for a dime what might fetch a dollar, maybe two or three. Even if the worst happened, even if he couldn't do a thing with them, Jay felt confident that he could drop the whole load for a quarter and walk away with 150 percent profit.

The next morning he was ready to get up and make a decision. But he couldn't get up, not without great pain—a backache riveted him to the mattress. Eventually, bent and sockless in his slippers, he hobbled to a chiropractor on 114th Street.

In the doctor's thermal Jacuzzi he began to thaw out.

"Lumbar misalignment and too much tension," the doctor said. He wrenched Jay's spine and kept him in his office all morning. Then he gave him the name of a chiropractically trained masseuse on 110th Street.

The next day, able to stand and walk, but fearful that the pain would return any second— and still on the fence about the swords—Jay met Lucy Fishman. She charged forty dollars for thirty minutes and confirmed what the doctor told him. The problem was the gap between his fourth and fifth vertebrae. Ms. Fishman wore a white shirtwaist dress. She looked like a nurse without a cap. Her hair was long and fluffy and twice it tickled his skin as she rubbed the empty spaces in his backbone.

"You should relax more," Lucy Fishman said, "or at least sit very straight while you're tense."

She asked him if this was an especially tense time, and he thought of the swords. "I have a chance to make a very lucrative but very risky business deal," he said. "I'm sure that's what's causing my back trouble."

Ms. Fishman stopped kneading and looked in his eyes.

"If you sell drugs get out of here," she said. He turned over and explained about the swords.

She apologized. Near the end of the massage she rubbed his ringless ring finger and asked him to call her sometime socially, if he wished.

Jay did, a week later, on the morning he bought the swords.

He had returned to the warehouse in the company of Abraham Huang. Once more Jay scanned the swords. Packed a thousand to a crate, there were 600 wooden boxes. He took one out of a crate and sliced the air. With Huang and James as witnesses, Jay Wilson cut his deal. He handed over a Bank of North Florida check for $60,000 and agreed to storage costs of $1,500 a month.

"Do you like my deal?" he asked Abraham Huang.

"I like," Huang said. "Now work begins."

That night at dinner Jay handed Lucy a sword. They were at a French restaurant on Eighty-sixth Street and between them they finished two bottles of wine. Lucy ordered lobster, which she cracked open with her solid strong fingers. As she ate, she explained the lobster's anatomy.

Even though the swords were all he talked about, Jay knew that Lucy Fishman was going to be more than a date. His lumbar region was connected to his heart.

"This is the biggest deal of my life," he said, "and you are a beautiful and intelligent woman. It feels like all at once I have a business and a personal life."

He leaned across the table to kiss her.

Later, in his bed, he massaged Lucy's back, but her specific directions discouraged him. He asked her to roll over. Face-to-face she was more a woman, less a technician. When he told her he was falling in love, she stopped talking about the density of spinal fluid.

"It's a new life," Jay whispered. "With you and the swords I really am starting over."

By the time the swords were locked into their new quarters in a John Street warehouse, Jay already knew how dead they were. He had called every distributor and broker listed in New York—no interest. Every one of them had already turned down the swords before Jay ever saw them.

"They're not worth the storage," a Brooklyn toy distributor told him. "I turned them down for a nickel. I wouldn't even take them for free."

At the end of his first month as the owner of 600,000 swords, Jay's back pain returned. But he was blessed with Lucy, who sat on the small of his back and realigned him as she listened to him lament his purchase. The $60,000 buy had exhausted his capital, but because of her his love was only beginning.

"Would you marry a bankrupt?" he asked her.

"Yes," Lucy said, "but I wouldn't lend him any money."

The masseuse said one thing, then did another. In the third month of their courtship, when Jay ran out of cash, she went to her savings account and paid the month's bill for storing the swords.

Lucy was cheerful about it. "It's like sending a kid to college."

Jay was full of love and guilt. "All those backrubs," he said, "all that good work to support my stupidity."

"You're not stupid," Lucy said.

"I threw away $60,000," he told Lucy, "nine years work. My youth."

"You're still young," she said. "You're just right for me."

He wanted to marry Lucy, but without money for a ring or a ceremony, he said nothing about his intentions.

When he had gone through his list of brokers and factors, when the Mets and the Yankees told him they had no interest in a Sword Day, when he had run up hundreds of dollars of bills on Lucy's phone calling Mexican and Venezuelan and even South African distributors, it suddenly occurred to Jay Wilson that he had been taken.

In a fit of rage he took a subway to Chinatown and pounded on the door of Huang's spacious loft. Mrs. Huang, frightened by the unusual man pounding on her steel door, buzzed for help. Cousin James, carrying a baseball bat, pinned Jay to the floor but relaxed when he recognized the man he'd driven around the West Side months before.

"East Side?" he asked, and put out his hand.

"Abraham Huang," Jay said. "Where is he?"

James led Jay down two creaky flights of stairs to a basement room where Huang sat watching an aquarium filled with brightly colored fish.

"My friend," Huang said as he rose to greet Jay.

"Friend, my ass. You set me up. You knew how much cash I had. You led me straight to those swords and set the price just at the top of my budget. Did you get the whole sixty?"

"No," Huang said, "only half."

"You bastard."

"Not bastard. Straight business."

"You knew nobody wanted them. You offered them all over town."

"All over world," Huang said. "Dime. Very cheap price. Require very big risk."

Cousin James brought in a pot of tea.

"You just took my money," Jay said. "You knew I'd never be able to sell."

"No. I knew Abraham Huang could not sell. Maybe Jay Wilson sell. This is business."

"Tea?" Cousin James said. "Later East Side?"

"I want my money," Jay said. "I'm in love. I want to get married, have a family. I was stupid to risk everything on one throw."

"Yes," Huang said, "swords stupid but love and family nice."

"I have no money."

"Most of world have no money. People marry, have children, live good."

Huang smiled, as friendly as ever. Jay Wilson, without a legal or moral leg to stand on, admitted his helplessness.

"It was my own fault," he said, "but I'll hate you until the day I die."

"Maybe not," Abraham Huang said. He bowed as Cousin James followed the visitor up the stairs.

Two months later, with the warehouse owner threatening to throw his 600 crates into the street, Jay, ten pounds lighter, sat at a wooden table at the corner of Amsterdam and Ninety-sixth Street. Unable to sell thousands or hundreds, he was now selling single swords, every day at another location. In two months of working New York street fairs, he had earned enough to pay for one month's storage. In two heavy canvas bags he carried ninety swords with him from fair to fair. He asked $3 apiece but often sold for less. He stopped eating lunch to save money, he looked for coins on the sidewalk, and though he had not done it yet, he started thinking about leaping over turnstiles to avoid paying subway fare. He pawned his Rolex watch, and as he suspected, Citibank offered him absolutely nothing for his 5 percent interest in the future of J & L Inc. When he could no longer pay his rent, he moved in with Lucy. Lucy still loved him.

"Forget the swords and get a job," she said. "You're a person like everyone else. You made a mistake. It's not the end of the world."

Jay knew she was right. He promised to forget the swords. He wanted just a month, six weeks—something might turn up. He chose the Fourth of July as the end.

"Promise?" Lucy asked.

Jay promised, and even in his despair, he knew how lucky he was to be teamed with this woman.

Since she worked close to the Amsterdam street fair, where he'd be today, Saturday, Lucy said she would bring him a lunch at Ninety-sixth Street. When she arrived at 12:30, he had sold only four swords. He had taken to carrying his money, mostly singles, in a wad in his left hand. Sometimes he wished that he had done that with the $60,000—kept it all in his hand in singles so he could feel how much it was before he squandered it on swords.

Jay held up four fingers. Lucy kissed his hand and gave him two peanut-butter sandwiches. She browsed for a few minutes, looking at the jewelry in the booth next to his.

The neighbor, an old hippie with a curly gray beard, did a good trade in antique earrings. Jay had seen him at other fairs, recognized him by his MAKE LOVE NOT WAR tattoo. His name was Chuck—he had introduced himself that morning as he laid out earrings and Jay stacked swords. Lucy browsed Chuck's table, and Jay watched the sun dip into her halter top. Her thin ribs glistened. Though he loved her, Jay Wilson, with his two bags of molded plastic swords, felt like a fool and a good-for-nothing beside her.

"Don't worry," Lucy said. "Eat your lunch. I'll see you at six."

To avoid embarrassing him, she didn't look back.

Scanning the street, Jay saw no potential customers. The temperature was already in the eighties—unseasonably warm for May. The winos were in the shade; the retirees who had been playing gin rummy folded their table. Only tired people pulling grocery carts walked past. The sun was so fierce that Jay put his samples back into the canvas bags to keep them from melting. On his scarred table the lunch bag sat alone. He considered eating one of the peanut-butter sandwiches, but, as usual, the thought of his 600,000 swords made him lose his appetite.

"Tough times, huh?" Chuck said.

"I used to have $60,000," Jay said. "Now I've got these."

"Hell," Chuck said, "in '67 I had a rainbow-colored van and four chicks. We had free acid and quadraphonic sound. Now I'm a grandfather." He pulled a picture from his nylon wallet. Jay gazed at a toddler.

"Nothing freakier than a kid, is there?" Chuck said.

Moved by his neighbor's past, Jay handed over the swords.

"Give 'em to your granddaughter," he said, "and to her friends."

"You should hang on to some," Chuck said as he accepted both canvas bags. "Sometimes they make a comeback, like the Confederate hat or the Mickey Mouse watch."

"Don't worry," Jay said, "I've kept a few." He gave Chuck his lunch, too. With his table now bare Jay put the wad of bills into his pocket and began to walk down Ninety-sixth Street.

"Hey," Chuck said, "don't give up. I know where you can get socks and blank tapes. They always use socks and tapes."

Jay waved and despite the heat began to jog uptown. Without ninety swords on his back he felt light and strong. At Ninety-ninth Street he began to run to the rhythm of a car alarm. People stared at him, wondering at his speed on such a day. At 110th Street he passed an Ethiopian parade. At 121st, though hardly panting, he paused for a line of people in red gowns with crosses emblazoned on their chests.

They were the faculty and students of the Union Theological Seminary. The seminary, a castle two blocks square, guarded the entrance to Grant's humble tomb. Jay jogged in place as he watched the graduation procession. The ministers-to-be, if armed with swords, could have passed for crusaders.

When the procession marched through the gates of the seminary, Jay, with nothing better to do, followed everyone into the cool auditorium and found a seat. The air-conditioning soothed him. But he felt hungry—he regretted giving his lunch to the earring seller. He rose to leave and get a sandwich but the ceremony was already in progress. The graduates, quiet as ghosts, were making their way down the aisles. An usher motioned for Jay to sit.

With no other choice, he stayed for graduation. He heard the coughs of the proud parents and the rustling of the ceremonial gowns. As the seminarians entered into the service of the Lord, Jay, lulled by the organ, fell into a quiet sleep. He awoke to the words of the commencement speaker.

Reverend Lamberts, a tall, thin man, touched the pages of his speech as if he were reading Braille; Jay, with the clarity of the awakened, heard everything. The Reverend described in detail an enormous undertaking of the church—the sponsorship of an International Day of Peace.

It took all of Jay's self-control to stay in his seat until the ceremony ended. When the graduates marched out, he rushed to the platform; he needed to know the date of the International Day of Peace.

At the end of the year, just before Christmas, on the International Day of Peace, people of goodwill assembled throughout the world. The president and other leaders of nations gave their approval to the event. Hindus and Muslims joined with the Federation of Churches and Synagogues. On a Sunday at noon eastern standard time, mankind condemned war.

Seventy-five thousand assembled in Tokyo's Olympic Stadium, 8,000 in London's Albert Hall. End zone to end zone they filled Soldier Field in Chicago, and 120,000 stood in the São Paulo soccer stadium. In Moscow and Kuala Lumpur, in select locations throughout the world, men and women made contemporary the words of the prophet. Nearly 600,000 blades, freshly stamped "Turn *Star Wars* into plough-shares," were raised and then dropped at exactly noon. Television throughout the world captured this historic event. Peace had not known such a day since 1945.

At two dollars apiece, the National Council of Churches considered the swords a bargain, a small price for international symbolism. Lucy Fishman, still pink as a bride, and Jay Wilson, an antiwar saint, stood among the crowd at Madison Square Garden and dropped their swords to enjoy, slightly more than anyone else on earth, the fruits of peace.

Stepdaughters

My wife sits beside me on our new leather couch. *Strength* is between us. "Who would have ever thought of this," Helen says. "I worried about boys, not about male hormones."

Our family life had been serene and moving toward joyful until Stephanie began shot-putting. Her eight-pound steel ball is now hammering all three of us. Stephanie is training for the state meet; Helen is fighting for her daughter's female body, and perhaps her soul. I am stepfather number three trying to stay on the sidelines.

If the battle over shot-putting was not destroying us, maybe I could laugh at it the way I now laugh at my fear of Harold. Two years ago, when I married Helen, I thought Harold, the real father, dead since Stephanie was three, would be the major obstacle in our new little family.

Steph kept a Harold shrine in her room: his glasses, some of his books, a few tapes of him reading stories to her, his college yearbooks, and a very thin family album started only a month or two before his death. Presiding over these scraps of her father's life Stephanie had hanging beside her bed a wall-size silkscreen of Harold's face.

The first time I saw that gigantic idolized father in her room I realized how impossible stepfathering would be.

I was timid and sentimental. For weeks I dreaded going near

Stephanie's room. I even thought of suggesting that we move but I knew she could just roll Harold up and carry him anywhere we might go. Then, one day, in the early stages of getting used to a teenager in my life, I noticed what I thought was a second Harold, a more ragged, menacing version of father on the wall opposite him.

"You like him?" Steph asked.

I didn't know how to answer.

"I'm not sure I do," she said, "but he was on sale for $7.98, so it was no big deal. "Most of the Steps are crazy about him."

The Steps are the Stepdaughters, a club Stephanie founded. He is Mick Jagger.

I burst out laughing and hugged my stepdaughter. A few weeks later I noticed that Steph had made an awkward twine pulley to raise and lower the image of her father. On nice days the sun streams in beneath Harold's eyebrows to illuminate Mick Jagger scowling across the room.

After that, I bought Stephanie a wall hanging, too, of a group called Genesis. I told her I hoped it would signify a beginning for the three of us.

She told me I was corny but she liked it. I started taking Stephanie places, too. I tried to take her to some event at least a couple of times a month.

"Al and Jerome ignored her," Helen told me, "and she doesn't even remember Harold."

Steph was thirteen then, the only daughter I would ever have. I took her to the ballet during the season, to the movies lots of times, and once to a track meet. Helen blames me for it.

"It's not the track meet alone," she says. "Secretly you condone the shot-putting, secretly you're on her side."

"I'm neutral."

"Nobody's neutral."

"It could be a lot worse."

"What could be worse?" She tosses *Strength* onto my lap.

"Go ahead, imagine her in this magazine next year surrounded by East German brutes."

"Helen, she's only fifteen, she's not going to be an Olympic athlete."

"Of course she will be," Helen says. "Look what she did with Stepdaughters, look at her grades, look at what that slimy coach told us."

Reluctantly, I had gone with Helen to threaten Coach Larry Zalenka. Helen wanted Stephanie off the team. Period. The coach, through only about thirty, was not a bit intimidated by Helen.

"Mrs. Harrison," he said, "if Steph was a man and in a popular sport she could turn pro at eighteen and become a millionaire. That's how good she is. She breathes shot-putting. You can't discourage something that strong."

"I can," Helen said, "and I will."

So far Helen has not succeeded in discouraging shot-putting, but it has become the only issue in our family. Helen had never heard of the event until last year. Even when Stephanie started carrying the big ball around the house as she chatted with us or helped set the table one-handed, Helen thought carrying the ball was some sort of exercise from *Jane Fonda's Workout Book*.

"I don't understand what you mean by throwing it," she told Stephanie. "You mean, you just throw it and that's all there is to it, no running around the bases or putting it through a basket, just throwing it anywhere?"

Stephanie tried to explain the complexity of the throw. She compared it to weight lifting, which took only a few seconds but was the most demanding of all sports.

"But what pleasure is there for you in practicing the same thing over and over, and what difference does it make if you throw it a few inches more or a few inches less?"

"I can't explain it, Mom, it just makes me feel better than anything else ever has."

At first, Helen considered the shot a heavy but harmless toy, like a Hula-Hoop or a yo-yo. She didn't begin to see how serious it was until Stephanie's new neck muscles began to be plainly visible.

Steph has never been petite. At school, her nickname since seventh grade has been Hulk. When Helen objected to the name Steph defended it.

"I'm five eight and I weigh one hundred fifty-five pounds," Stephanie said. "I'm not the kind of girl who is going to be called Cutie Pie. Anyway, I like being strong. I don't see why I should be ashamed of it."

In spite of her size Stephanie had not seemed exceptionally strong until she began her serious training about six months ago.

Now, Steph is fifteen, so is her neck. It surprises you sliding out from under her thin delicate face, as thin and delicate as Helen's own face. The neck is an introduction to Stephanie's powerful shoulders and upper arms, which descend into thin wrists and long symmetrical fingers. It almost looks as if there are two Stephanies, one a somewhat delicate girl, the other a bulky Steph placed on top but not quite filling in all the open spaces.

Helen knew something was happening to Steph. She suggested that Stephanie grow her hair longer or stop wearing turtleneck blouses. Then, one morning on the *Today* show Helen watched a report on drug use by female athletes. Steph had already gone to school.

Helen drove to St. James Academy in her housecoat and had Stephanie summoned from homeroom. They sat in Helen's car in front of the school. Helen accused her daughter of taking male hormones.

"I knew it as soon as I saw the report on TV. I knew something had changed you and now I understand." Helen wept against the steering column.

Stephanie denied it.

"I do weights and dynamic tension, that's all, just Nautilus. Mom, I'm not crazy, I wouldn't take drugs like that. I don't even smoke grass. You can ask Jackie or any of the Steps if you don't believe me."

Helen does not believe her, though there is no evidence against Stephanie, only her body. She is getting stronger right before our eyes. Of course, she works at it during all her waking hours. At night the shot lies on the pillow beside her.

She does dynamic tension, pitting muscle groups against each other, while she studies.

"Do you do it in school, too?" Helen asks.

"Yes, nobody can tell most of the time and it doesn't get in the way. I don't do it in Chem lab or when I'm giving an oral report or something like that, just when I'm sitting quietly reading or listening."

Steph was doing dynamic tension at the dinner table, too, until Helen banned it, but since the *Today* report Helen has declared total war on shot-putting. Stephanie is standing up for her right to be big and strong and throw the steel ball as far as she can.

They are both strong-minded women. When I was dating Helen I admired the way mother and daughter worked together starting the Stepdaughters. Stephanie lobbied parents and teachers as if she were a thirteen-year-old union organizer. She and Jackie prepared a membership pamphlet and designed a T-shirt logo.

Several parents called Helen to complain about a club of stepdaughters discussing intimate family details without any adult supervision. Helen defended her daughter then as wholly as she now attacks Stephanie's shot-putting.

"All the girls were just sitting around and complaining," Steph told me. "Jackie's mother and father have each been married twice and her father's second wife has four stepchildren of her own. Once, in the line at the supermarket, all three girls ahead of her were Jackie's stepsisters and she hardly knew them. She said she would need a computer just to keep track of who was talking to who. One day we were complaining about how stupid all the school clubs were—who wants to be in Latin Club or Future Teachers, so I thought, "What about a stepdaughters club?" When I told Mom she said it could become the Alcoholics Anonymous of the new century."

One of the first things I ever did with Steph was to drive her to a Stepdaughters meeting. The girls meet at the public library on Friday night. Wisely, they realized the necessity for a public meeting place. A house, anybody's house, would put them at the mercy of family life. I decided to wait for her in the car across the street.

I noticed that after the meeting the girls loitered on the tall steps of the library. Teenage boys in their parents' cars circled the library as if waiting for the sudden onset of moral dehydration.

"They're a drag," Stephanie told me later. "One of the things we talk about in Stepdaughters is that there is no Mr. Right and there's no perfect therapist either."

Jackie, whom I met that night, told me she thought Steph would become a senator or at least go around the country making speeches and establishing Stepdaughters franchises like Weight Watchers and Speedreaders all over the country.

Helen had equally ambitious hopes for her daughter's future.

"Of course," she said, "I want her to be happy. I told her that and I told the coach and the psychiatrist the same thing."

"'Let her assert herself,' that silly psychiatrist said, 'let her do what she chooses.'

"I reminded him that one of his colleagues told Mr. and Mrs. Hinckley the same thing a few weeks before their son went out to shoot President Reagan."

"That's not exactly right," I told her.

"It's close enough. All I'm trying to tell you is the simple fact that there is no professional I can turn to in this crisis. For almost anything else you can think of there is a hot line or a UN agency or a readathon. All the miserable have company and sympathy. I have to sit alone and watch my daughter, my beautiful Stephanie, do dynamic tension to her neck and arms. Every morning while she chews her toast I look to see if the facial hair has started to grow."

I try to put my arms around Helen but she resists comfort. She has always looked facts in the face. She survived her husband's early death and then two bad marriages. On her way to becoming a successful executive, she started as a young widow selling Avon products door to door.

When I told Helen I wanted to marry her she asked for some time to think about it. Two days later she gave me a computer printout based on Prudential Insurance Company statistics that predicted the likelihood of everything from breast cancer to senility in her person during the next twenty-five years.

"I'm forty-one," she said, "I can't treat getting married as a honeymoon. You should know what you're getting into."

"Maybe I should give you my computer breakdown too."

"I have it." Out of her purse she produced the melancholy table of my projected decline. "This tells us more about love than music and moonlight do. This is what's coming for both of us—alone or together is the question."

After reading the insurance projections, I asked for a few days, then I decided—together. The tables were for death and disease, they left out love, health, and happiness, the things you seek in life. I told her the tables had nothing to do with marriage.

"I know," she said, "I've just learned to look at the bleakness first."

For two years Helen, Steph, and I were oblivious of statistical disaster. We were in love with one another and with our little unit, a functioning family, so new to each of us. Now an eight-pound steel ball seemed as dangerous as another woman, a runaway, or financial ruin, the less exotic tragedies of other families.

"You can't blame puberty," Helen said. "I wish it was something that simple, that physical." She looked at me in all sincerity.

"Would you break her wrist or dislocate it or something?" Finally Helen started to cry. For two months form alone carried the day; finally Helen had reached the end of her good manners.

In order to understand her objection to shot-putting, you have to understand the kind of woman Helen is. In almost every way she is as open-minded and straightforward as she can be. When we met she told me she was lonesome and sensual and intelligent. She said she had no patience for fools. She described herself accurately. When depression awakened her at 4 AM, she told me, she arose to read from the novels of Balzac. Helen rarely looks backward.

After Jerome, her second bad marriage, she went to a behavioral psychologist. From him she learned that she was not able to profit from the study of her past.

I told her that a year from now the shot-putting might seem no big deal.

"A year from now," she said, "I could be dead and Bin Laden could be ruling the world. I'm only interested in today."

From the start of our romance I admired her unrelenting honesty. She said that she was skeptical about love but admitted great needs and great pleasures as they arose.

"You love me because I'm a beautiful woman," she said. "I'm not speaking of vanity, you know that: I'm telling you that you love me because I am a woman, because I'm not what you are. Every woman, no matter how weak, no matter how abused, understands her importance in the world because she is a woman. Men don't have that feeling. They don't need it, they have everything else.

"No matter how ridiculous it seems, beauty and femininity are necessities. When I was an Avon lady I would spend hours with ugly women, disfigured women. They took me into their homes. We drank coffee and talked about Pan-Cake makeup and eye shadow and blush and fragrance. A few of my ten-dollar products made all the difference to them. I was never ashamed of being an Avon lady. I think their work is more important than IBM.

"There are women who lose their femininity. Then they have nothing because they're not men either, and they're not children, though they often act as if they are. I'm seeing that happen to Steph right before my eyes. Just while she is blossoming in puberty, she is dewomanizing herself. I would rather have her be a Moonie or a cocaine addict, you can recover from those things. If she loses the core of being a woman, then she'll end up playing touch football and drinking beer in some trailer park in New Mexico—or worse."

Stephanie is unmoved by this argument.

"You just want me to have ruddy cheeks," she says, "and giggle when boys call and worry about my periods. I don't have to do any of those things. That's an act, what girls are supposed to be like. You should know better, you helped me start Stepdaughters, you should want me to tell you my true feelings."

"Stephanie, my love, you know I want you to tell me your true feelings."

"My truest feeling is that I want to throw the shot as far as possible, maybe sixty feet."

Helen has removed all drugs from the house; there are no aspirins, no antihistamines, no cold tablets. She also allows Stephanie no seconds at dinner. In fact, she is cooking such small portions that all three of us leave the table hungry. Still, Stephanie's neck thrives, her shoulders grow like breasts. She has also switched her everyday shoes from penny loafers to gray climbing shoes in order to strengthen her ankles for her gliding technique.

When Stephanie and I are alone she does talk to me about her passion.

"It's not just strength," she tells me, "it's mostly the feel of it, the rhythm. Some people think it's shoulder and wrist—not true, anybody can get shoulders and wrists. It's the neck that's crucial."

She asks me very matter-of-factly if I'm going to divorce Helen because of the shot-putting dispute.

"That's between your mother and you. Why should that lead to a divorce between Helen and me?"

"Well, it can't be much fun for you hanging around the two of us always at each other."

Like Helen, she has a knack for the bleak truth.

"You can just pack up whenever you want. You don't have to put up with us. You must know by now that this is not going to stop. After the state meet I start training for the regionals and then I'm going for all the Olympic trials. Coach says you peak at about eighteen. I'm going to give it everything I've got for the next three years and you can bet that Mom's going to fight me every inch. Life around this house is not going to be a picnic."

She holds an imaginary ball against her neck, turns her back to me, and begins to practice her glide technique. She leans backward on her right leg, points her left leg at the fireplace, and takes one powerful hop across the white carpet. When she lets go, her hips lead, then her arm, her head, and her neck snap up in a strong united motion.

As I watch Stephanie constantly repeating her approach and throwing motion, I think of her girlfriends, that hypnotic clan of stepdaughters: Ellen, with her belt made of lacquered Xerox copies of alimony checks; Carol, who tells all adults she just wants to be left alone—forever; Harriet, who talks constantly of wanting to take long silent horseback rides through fields of wildflowers. I think of these pale followers of my shot-putting Stephanie, these youngsters who have shriveled into the dimensions that loneliness allows them.

Not Stephanie. With her eyes closed and the imaginary ball pressed against her neck she is in the trance of hope. Her father is a window shade, her previous stepfathers long gone, her mother destined to misunderstand the beauty of Stephanie's strength. As Stephanie rocks on her back leg, eyes closed, lips pressed tight, I see that shot-putting is as solemn as prayer. She has a lot to throw away, this stepdaughter of mine; in eight-pound chunks she might be able to manage it, maybe all the way to the Olympics.

When she opens her eyes I am standing across the room imitating her stance. Stephanie laughs.

"At least take off your tie," she says. "Nobody shot-puts in a tie."

Even before I begin my arm feels sore. My legs are fifty—I remember the insurance company table. I feel the cholesterol, the blood pressure, the statistical saga of a tired body that must gear itself up each day for a 150-pound throw against the darkness. Yet, I feel as filled with hope and prayer as she is.

Steph and I point our left feet at one another like swordsmen in a Douglas Fairbanks movie.

"On three," she says. And we begin.

Sized Up

All over the place, people much younger were sprouting diseases Ferguson had never heard of. Yet at forty-six, and not in love, he wanted a child. This was supposed to happen only to women, but here he was, stewing in male hormones and mushy every time he heard a baby cry.

For the last few months it had been worse than ever. Right next door he listened in on family life. Before Anthony was born, Ferguson barely spoke to Joan or Bob in the elevator. He heard them sometimes in the bedroom, white noise, a blur, none of his business. But when Anthony shrieked at 3 AM and Joan and Bob argued about who would get out of bed, Ferguson wanted to pound on the wall and volunteer. He had done no more than tickle the baby's fat chin one day in front of the building, but he listened so well and longed for an infant so profoundly that he almost believed that Anthony, a tiny wizard so close to the secrets of life, cried for the tender arms of Ferguson, his neighbor, a seller of industrial equipment.

As he listened through the wall to the regular suspiration of Anthony nursing, Ferguson, dense with memory, considered his own lost opportunities. Marriage was the first. Sally, a dancer, never wanted children, had been absolutely honest about it since the start. When they divorced he was only thirty-five, still had taut skin, a reasonably full head of hair, and what had he done with his thirties, four years with Lisa, who had had to give up her pustular ovaries while still an undergraduate. And then Nancy, the mistake of his forties—so far.

Through the wall Anthony shrieked, and Mommy, whom Ferguson imagined in milk beside her infant, came running from the kitchen.

"Mommy's been on the phone, sweetheart, did your dolly fall out of bed? There, Mommy will pick him up."

Ferguson heard Joan squeeze the toy and recognized from the cavities of the rubber doll the sounds he had mistaken for nursing. Still, he did not feel cheated. A baby and a rubber doll were also an interesting couple, and whether he heard them or not, Ferguson knew that a mother and child were only a thin wall away. The father he could have done without.

Bob, a veterinarian, usually carried a gerbil in his shirt pocket. On the elevator the little rodent peeked out as if to demand that the button for his floor be pushed. He nibbled at Bob while Bob ascended toward the bliss of his own home. Sometimes through the wall Ferguson heard the gerbil running his circular path and worried that the animal might gnaw at Anthony's toes, but Ferguson said nothing. The family next door were strangers, and Bob, that friend to beasts, turned away from Ferguson's meager efforts at camaraderie. Recently, when they met at Safeway, the veterinarian talked shock absorbers. "Those strollers should have them," he said. "Even the sidewalks are so damned bumpy, but I guess the babies don't mind after all those months in the oven."

"The womb," Ferguson reminded the doctor, "is not an oven."

"You sound like you know something about that."

Ferguson hoped the rodent would burrow through Bob's pocket and chew away at his neighbor's stony heart. But he smiled, a friendly shopper on a Sunday morning.

"Not much. Never had a child."

"A lot of work."

"I'll bet it is."

At the exit, Ferguson collided with the entrance door, looked at himself for two seconds in the glass, then hurdled the guard rail and left on the run.

At home he moped. From his window he could see the park where joggers spread like a fungus. Usually he was one of them. This he had learned from almost half a century of life, how to take one step after another for three to six miles, how to talk to a purchasing agent about a milling machine, how to fall asleep at ten in front of his TV.

With Nancy he thought his life as a father was going to begin. He was forty then, maybe forty-one, but Nancy, a dark-eyed realist, looked at her life and found no room for children or Ferguson. He wanted to marry her. They could have had a kindergartner already, maybe a preschooler as well.

Nancy considered their marriage for months. At the movies, as he reached for the popcorn she held, Ferguson used to imagine the box of swollen grains as her rising belly. He'd stroked the kernels, could barely chew, felt bereft when she put the buttery bucket underneath her seat.

"I tried," Nancy told him. "For weeks I lay down flat every night, no pillow, no sheet. I'd look at myself and try to imagine my pregnant body and our life together. Sometimes it was very sweet. Sometimes I'd fall into a light sleep and feel the little fingers clutching my hair. And I know what a kind man you are, what a good father you'd be. Sometimes I'd think, this is really me, I could be a mother. Then you know what happens? I get up and take my pill, and it's over. It just can't be, Fergy, I know myself too well. The best thing about me, no matter what's happened, is that I've always stayed a size 6."

He should have known even as Nancy said it that size was the key, but it took one more torturous episode, one more snag of flesh and spirit before Ferguson got the message.

Madeline, la petite, spelled it out. With her, last year, it was not love, not another Nancy, thank God, but good company, fun, more than he'd had in years. He knew Madeline didn't want marriage so he proposed a legal agreement. He would bind himself to 50 percent responsibility for everything, not just money. He would have said 100 percent, but what mother wants to be a mere service? He would have a lawyer create the document, he would put the money in trust. In the future they could, of course, consider marriage.

Madeline thought it over, even went to her boss to discuss maternity leave, but a working stewardess, she decided, couldn't be a reliable mother to an infant.

"By the time I stopped missing my baby, meal service would be over, and nobody would understand why I was crying, and if I explained, I'd have to spend the rest of the flight listening to some guy with a computer in his lap telling me about his terrific children before he invited me to his hotel."

Madeline had five more years before her pension fund would be vested. Then, at thirty-five, she would try for a family.

"I know there's a risk if I wait too long. To me there's a risk, anyway. My bone structure is just right for the aisles of a 737, but for babies you need hips, thighs, breasts. If you want babies, Ferguson, look for a different type of woman, look for an earth mother."

As soon as she said it Ferguson knew Madeline had given him the key to his failures. He had fallen in love with the same woman, virtually the same dress size, over and over. Sally, Lisa, Nancy, they could have shared closets—size 6s, and then tiny Madeline, barely a 4. He was going backward. Babies came from flesh, and when Ferguson considered his past, it was clear to him that he had always been running from flesh. His entire life now seemed like a membership in a health studio. Sally a dancer, Lisa a vegetarian, Nancy holding on to size 6 as if it were God's name, Madeline a sprite of the air . . . there had been little weight, no woman who anchored herself and him with a body. In his time Ferguson had loved mannequins, given birth to splinters. Of course, he was blind to it, how could it be otherwise? He had grown to middle age in the era of the healthy. While he married, divorced, courted slender women, and sold industrial tools, the flesh had melted away from his generation. Gray-haired women in leotards shopped for sprouts, executives threw away their cigars and ran marathons.

What happened to softness, to latitude? Where were the stout ladies like his grandma, who wore dresses with large flowers and talked Polish on street corners?

With new eyes Ferguson made up his mind to seek flesh, and he knew where to look. There were many choices, but he wanted a place unfamiliar. He drove miles, watched nature change and street signs grow sparse. Finally, amid a grove of oak trees, he came upon the dappled splendor of Greyhill Mall. Wind chimes greeted him at the door, and the sounds of birds and children made it seem like Paradise on the enclosed marble boulevard.

Ferguson, already dazed by his new resolve, looked in wonder at the everyday, a mall on Saturday afternoon. The centerpiece of the mall was an aviary, and for it the owners of Greyhill had sought out jungle birds to complement the lush indoor foliage. Wisecracking parrots groomed themselves near the skylight. Macaws hummed like old-timers on their front porches. On the ground, two-year-old children still learning what legs and arms can do reached toward the aviary, hoping to tear a feather from the birdies.

"No, no," Ferguson heard a gentle father say to a reaching curly-haired boy, or maybe it was a girl. "Birdie has to stay in cage. Birdie flies. Birdie sings."

"Birdie," said the child, opening his hands. "Birdie."

"No," the father said.

The child ran to mother, hid his face against her wool skirt. Ferguson had never seen a more perfect instinct.

Dads, like Bob the veterinarian, pushed foldable strollers filled with rosy-cheeked treasure as casually as Ferguson had guided his Chevy through the light traffic.

Mothers, fathers, children, out in the mall, the most human stuff. It looked so easy for everyone else, and it must have been. People fell in love, mated. Like every species they brought forth what they brought forth—fruit, seeds, pods, eggs, cells, genes, chromosomes. As Ferguson looked on from his bench near the aviary, the whole moist swarm of biology lurched in waves between Sears at one end of the mall and Penney's at the other.

Ferguson alone, but in the middle of it all, tried to keep his wits about him as he scanned the crowd for full-figured women.

If he could trust his senses, and if this Saturday was like any other, and he was at Greyhill and not in the suburbs of heaven, then full-figured women were as abundant here as on the walls of an art museum. If Ferguson had only shopped here, he might have discovered the shape of life sooner and been out back right now raising bicycle seats for nine-year-olds or coaching first base for Little Leaguers.

A woman with hips in faded dungarees who was wiping ice cream from her daughter's chin almost brought tears to Ferguson's eyes. She does this every day, he thought, many times, wipes lips, cleans ears, straps the little one in the car seat, tells bedtime stories, purées vegetables, and has a husband, too, probably someone who comes home from work to the noisy music of this little girl, and others, and pets, and friends, and he has all this, the absolutely packed world of his own house, because years ago, while Ferguson was drawn to bone, this man and the whole wise happy world of fathers had chosen flesh.

Only years of good manners and the sense that he might be going mad kept Ferguson from approaching this woman, wiping the wisps of hair from her forehead as carefully as she had tended to her daughter's chin, and asking mother and child to run away with him. The father no doubt would find another wife, do it all over again without missing a beat. Ferguson would cherish the child, treat her better than if she was his own. A little boy joined the woman, began to push his sister's stroller. The rich get richer, Ferguson thought. The mother arose from her cleansing crouch, her thighs rubbing together as she hustled to catch up with her children.

Ferguson's pulse beat the wedding march. He wanted a wife and a child now, this afternoon. He was standing on the bench beneath the aviary, ready to pound his chest like a gorilla and cry out, "Wench, wife, anybody, come to me." He would wait only until closing time. A passing clergyman would perform the ceremony. Ferguson scanned the shoppers for clerical collars. A woman in black might have been a nun, but her headphones made it unlikely.

"Mister," a boy said to Ferguson, "you're scaring the birds."

The boy pointed at the parrots. They were shivering at the top of the aviary. Their beaks were blue. Ferguson was standing on the bench, but he had not yelled, not pounded his chest, not yet. The boy was wearing knee-length Hawaiian shorts and had a brush cut. He looked the way Ferguson remembered himself looking in 1952, when his father told him so solemnly that General Eisenhower had saved the country once and would do it again. Ferguson remembered Ike, his father's hero and his, too, at twelve. Ike smiling and bald, swinging a golf club, his thumbs pointing at his ear.

"Leave 'em alone," the boy said, "you're not supposed to pester the birds."

"I'm not pestering," Ferguson said, "just looking."

On his tiptoes, his nose against the wire, what he saw was not the birds but his own face in the birds' mirror. Ferguson, bald as Eisenhower, pale as Nixon, a man wild for the tiniest republic, a family.

"I'm gonna call a cop," the boy said.

Ferguson was looking straight up at the second level of the aviary, itself a mall with birdish attractions—seeds, flowers, vegetables, grains, an attractive decor probably done by a specialist in bird architecture. The underbellies of the exotic species blazed in yellows and dark blues. The boy, probably a member of the Audubon Society, kept his eyes on Ferguson, and Ferguson eyed the parrots. It was a standoff.

Ferguson surprised himself by yelling "Eisenhower" to the parrots before he merged with the shoppers heading for the escalators.

From the second level he looked out at joggers, like sentries circling the parking lot, while moms, dads, and kids slipped through to hit Sears or get a haircut or just parade through the enclosed space before Ferguson, a witness.

He found what he sought on 2 West, tucked between State Farm and a Hallmark shop. There Ferguson loitered, leaned leftward as if to convince passersby that he was a family man thinking things over carefully before he stepped into State Farm for a free insurance checkup. "Coverage okay?" he would ask. "Up to date? Or maybe I should add a college education for two, a payment on a mobile home." For himself Ferguson already had plenty. His retirement plan was as secure as age itself. Industrial equipment took care of its own.

While he pretended insurance, his eyes scanned Harriet's electronic doorway. The women came in pairs, as if the shop were an ark, and he did not notice that the customers were any bulkier than the throng on the first level shopping beneath the aviary. When he heard a voice, Ferguson thought it must be the boy again, but it was a female, past childbearing age, yet handsome, and modest in the way that she approached him.

"Excuse me, sir, do you want to use the phone or something? Of course you're welcome to stand here. But is there anything I can do, maybe direct you somewhere?"

"No, I'm just standing in front of Harriet's," Ferguson said, "that's about it."

"I know," she said. "I'm Harriet. Why not come in?" She extended her hand. Ferguson liked the feel of it, heftier than his own, but delicate, too, not pulling him toward the store, just a hello, a grip of friendship, none of the aggressive let's-get-this-over-with-and-get-down-to-business greeting he was accustomed to in sales.

"You have a lovely store," said Ferguson.

"It's even nicer inside. Are you interested in a gift for someone?"

Ferguson, wishing he could lie, said nothing.

"I know," Harriet said. "Men have trouble buying little things, especially for big women. It's okay, that's one of the things we're here for. We've got a complete line of lingerie, and believe me, it's a lot easier here than at a department store. Come on in, there's no obligation."

He followed her. Inside were racks of dresses and a few mirrors, nothing exotic, only garments.

"I'm just looking," Ferguson said.

"Then what can I show you?"

Already where he wanted to be, Ferguson, feeling the courage accrued from his wasted years, told the truth.

"I'm looking at the women."

Harriet stopped among the nighties.

"I know that some men put ads in the newspapers for cripples or fat people, but you don't seem like a sicko."

"I'm not, I'm not," Ferguson said, wondering if he was even as he denied. He told Harriet his repetitions of size 6s and the longing he felt now for a fuller life with a fuller-figured woman.

She listened, he couldn't know whether in wonder or in judgment.

"How did you find Harriet's?" she asked.

"The Yellow Pages—I looked under large sizes. The big-men's stores take out half-page ads showing husky guys hooking their thumbs into their suspenders. For women they don't even use boldface type. I needed a magnifying glass to make sure I got the right address. My eyes aren't as good as they used to be."

"But your brain is working. You understand now why I'm in business. In department stores, large women are ashamed. I've got customers so beautiful that you'd think Jesus had kissed them, and yet they're embarrassed to walk into a dressing room with a size 18. Even here, most of my business is mail order. Size turns young women into hermits. When I see a crocheted tablecloth I can hardly stand to look at it. I know that big hands have turned those tiny stitches. Yessir, mister, you're onto something, weirdo or not. You're okay in my book."

Harriet's book, as it happened, was an eleven-county mailing list. In her storeroom, among last year's styles, which to Ferguson looked exactly like this year's styles, Harriet opened her book and sought, not by size alone, the right customer. She brewed herbal tea on a hot plate and considered driving distance, too, though Ferguson, accustomed to travel in his work, considered eleven counties a neighborhood.

"This is new to me," Harriet said, "so I'm being careful. And believe me, my mailing list is not for sale, I don't care if you're the United Fund. It's got to be someone I've seen recently. Time, you know, changes everything. I might give you a name who's lost a hundred pounds in six months."

My luck, Ferguson thought.

As Harriet skimmed alphabetically by county, Ferguson wondered if he could actually be drawn to a full-figured woman. His new attitude made sense, but would his heart and limbs and organs agree? Harriet, a reader of minds as well as lists, asked, "Have you ever dated a large woman?"

"No."

"What about your mom, sisters, cousins, any of them oversized?"

"An only child," Ferguson said. Then he recalled his grandmother. "She was big, yes, and wonderful."

Of course. He had loved his grandmother and accompanied her to buy millinery, which always surprised him by being just a hat. Yes, his grandmother, dead since he was sixteen, but a big solid woman, still a presence in his life even thirty years later, reaching across a generation to remind her grandson in Harriet's tiny office that once he had known and loved a woman of size. For her, he decided on the spot, he would name the first child.

"Here's a possibility," Harriet said. She dropped a page of computer printouts in front of him. There were at least sixty or seventy names. All Ferguson knew of his possibility was middle of the alphabet.

When Harriet raised her eyes from the printout she wrote a name on yellow memo-pad paper with a sticky back. She pressed it onto Ferguson's shirt above his heart.

"Why her?" Ferguson asked.

"Intuition."

Ferguson lowered his eyes, read the name upside down.

"Harriet," he said, "I don't know how to thank you."

"Maybe," she said, "you won't."

Ferguson spent the week awaiting his date, remembering the females he used to admire as a boy—the stars in his mother's movie magazines, Dorothy Lamour, Hedy Lamarr, Lana Turner, and his own first crush, Margaret O'Brien, a dark-haired teenager who loved horses. These were what women were like before he knew what women were like, and there was always his mother, glamorous to her son in a green felt hat with a curved feather. Maybe that was where the size 6 business started. Though he had no memory of his mother ever mentioning her size, he recalled with great clarity certain Saturday afternoons at the seamstress's house, Mrs. Duess, her German accent almost sharp enough to cut the rayons and cottons his mother brought to her for salvation. "This one, Mrs. Duess, would be just right if you could put a dart on either side."

His mother cooed over Mrs. Duess, valued her even though the war was still a fresh memory, and Mrs. Duess felt herself a suspect in the Midwest.

Ferguson sat on a velveteen couch and nibbled homemade strudel while the seamstress worked and his mother talked, and together they remade the clothes that Aunt Rachel, who shopped at Saks Fifth Avenue, passed down or the garments that his mother, with a better eye for price than size, had picked up with the money that she told herself and her little boy was her bonus for never having a cleaning lady.

Could that be where it all started, on the couch watching the seamstress's fingers spreading the material while the needle did its narrow job? He remembered the gooseberry filling of the strudel leaking onto his fingers, the care he took to keep the stains off the couch while he watched Mrs. Duess's foot control the Singer, and his mother, nervous about mistakes, overpraising the golden hands that were contributing, so inexpensively, to her own beauty. And then the trying-on, when they sent him into the hallway to wait, and he looked at the words *Otis Elevator* until his mother opened the door, looking radiant, and Mrs. Duess seemed like a fairy godmother in the background, watching style and fit and good clean hemlines.

Maybe in Mrs. Duess's living room he had learned from his mother the unspoken commandment of attraction: Thou shalt have no heavy-set women before me. So Sally and Lisa and Nancy and the scores of casual dates, had they all been formed by Mrs. Duess and his mother? Had his future been cut from a bargain cloth purchased when he was seven years old and still in love with his mother?

No more. Ferguson, a good salesman even when capital spending was down, found it impossible to concentrate on his appointments. He had an almost brand-new shear that could cut four tons of sheet metal in an hour and a possible customer for it in Dayton, Ohio, but equipment was not on his mind.

Harriet called him at his office. "I'm worried," she said, "that I did something I shouldn't have done. I don't even know you. What is it you want?"

Ferguson closed his door so the office wouldn't hear. It also gave him a few seconds to think. A wife and a child were only part of the answer. You didn't have to be Harriet to know that smaller women also give birth.

"You walked into my store," Harriet said, "and I pointed you to a person whom I adore, and I don't know if I should have done it. With certain women a date is not just a date, do you know what I mean? Lives can be bitter forever after one casual rejection. What do you want, Ferguson? Don't play."

"I'm not playing," he said, "I want a change, a difference. I want to open up, Harriet, be bigger myself. Does it make any sense?"

"A man is a flower, too," Harriet said.

When he hung up Ferguson wasn't so sure. Maybe a flower, maybe a stained fabric, a pattern cut but not used.

Part dishrag, part flower, the salesman on a Saturday night in April drove to Clinton County to meet Lil, who on the phone sounded as lively as the aviary at the Greyhill Mall.

The town she lived in was too small for a Wal-Mart. Ferguson circled through once, then parked at the side of the road. Not sure how long it would take him, he had started out early. Now he had an hour's wait. He drove again to the center of town, scouting for a place to have dinner. He found parking meters and a movie theater, but for dinner the choice looked like McDonald's, Denny's, or Big Boy.

As he waited he drank coffee at Big Boy, choosing it for its spacious booths and indirect lighting.

Now, less than an hour from her, Ferguson in the restaurant let Lil blossom in his imagination. They would enter this booth, she sliding in ahead of him, the waitress recognizing Ferguson, already liking him because of his big tip only a few minutes ago. And Lil, a dainty eater as he expected, would tell him that this was her first date in seven years. She had not given up on life, only on men. She had girlfriends who would walk through fire for her, a boss who worshiped her, and Harriet, who sent her clothes and now a date. A toast to Harriet, to the mall, to the curiosity that had led him to a small town, a large woman, a new beginning.

When he mentioned a child Lil would say, "Not so fast, we just met. I may be overweight, but I'm not crazy."

And he, Ferguson, on a Saturday night, finishing his coffee and about to pick up a rural woman, was he a fool to expect more than he had? Was a playpen just a noisier version of a Mercedes? His youth was gone, his middle age fleeing. All the little Fergusons-that-might-have-been added up only to him on a red vinyl seat looking at booths full of teenagers.

When he got to his car five minutes before date time, Ferguson gunned the engine, not sure if he would stop at 314 Virginia Avenue or speed back to his own apartment, forget this quest, and sip alone from his half glass of the water of life.

In front of Lil's house, Ferguson, his foot on both the brake and accelerator, looked into an open door. Framed by the light within, Lil waited. Her relatives moved across his line of vision. She wore light blue, no flowers, and her hair, brown and wavy, touched the tops of her shoulders.

Ferguson saw no size, just a woman as nervous as he was, wondering what might happen. In the small-town quiet he heard birds, though it might have been radios.

Much later, and to his great surprise, Ferguson found a baby, himself.

He nuzzled Lil, caressed her solid shoulder.

"All me," she said, "big as life." Ferguson, still a baby, but growing very fast, reached for it.

Threads

In a Buenos Aires warehouse, only a few blocks from the landing where travelers awaited the ferry to Punta del Este, Ira Silvers of Baltimore examined a replica of the interior of his Charles Street apartment. It was not an exact copy, but close, down to a version of his fuzzy green sofa.

In Baltimore, Ira would be on that sofa, one foot over the worn back. Here it was occupied by the actor Emile Delgado, who sipped sweetened coffee as he went over his lines.

Ira did not understand the Spanish script, but as he roamed the set, every once in a while he heard his untranslated name. He heard it as one word: Irasilvers. In the midst of all the Spanish it sounded as patriotic as "The Star-Spangled Banner."

Even though the strike began at noon, the actors thought it would be over in a few hours. Those already in costume kept their antennae and aluminum foil vests in place. The camera crew and the technicians, already on strike, didn't leave. They were out front, in the trailer of a semi truck playing blackjack while they waited for permission to return to work.

Silvers, on his second day in Argentina, didn't mind the strike. He enjoyed the breeze as he looked across the wide Rio de la Plata, toward Montevideo.

Only ten days ago, he had been lying on his original couch watching the Orioles in the midst of a record losing streak when Feldman called, offering him two hundred dollars a day to stand by in case they needed new material during the shooting of *Filth.*

Ira didn't even know the film was going to be made. A year ago Feldman had run across Ira's story and had paid Silvers a flat fee, ten thousand dollars, for a ninety-seven-page film script. Feldman himself translated it into Spanish.

"I'm not Warner Brothers or Twentieth Century–Fox," Feldman told the surprised writer. "I make movies on less than their catering budgets, but below the equator, people think Victor Feldman is Cecil B. DeMille."

Silvers wrote the screenplay in a week, pocketed the fee, and considered himself the luckiest man on earth. When the producer called a year later, during the seventh inning of a 4-0 loss to the Tigers, Ira was too stunned to answer.

Feldman mistook surprise for greed.

"Two hundred dollars a day is all I pay the stars," the producer reminded him, "and we can do this without you. You're like an insurance policy. In case something doesn't work you write out a new scene or two and I put it into Spanish on the spot. We don't even have to type out scripts. Exact words don't make any difference."

Silvers accepted, and here he was, in midafternoon of shooting day. The cast was edgy after four hours of waiting, when Feldman entered the warehouse and called everyone together.

"Under the military government," the producer said, "I made twelve films. I put Argentina on the movie map. Now they torture me with taxes, and permits, and every couple of months, a strike. Well, they've jacked Victor Feldman around once too often."

Emile Delgado, who now held his antennae in his hands, asked when the shooting would begin.

"When somebody who knows how to run things takes over this country. Believe me, I told the minister of commerce a year ago that Feldman Productions did not have to stay in Buenos Aires. I reminded him that there is Santiago de Chile."

As the actors dispersed, Feldman called the writer aside.

"Check with the hotel every day," he told Ira. "I'll leave you a message. In the meantime, enjoy it. You're on a paid vacation. See if you can write a script for a quick coup to bring the generals back."

The writer had other business. In his briefcase next to the annotated screenplay were the letters regarding his Uncle Carlos. Two years late, the nephew arrived in Buenos Aires. Carlos had died in 1986. The year of his death was the only thing Ira knew about his uncle. Ira's late father, Howard, told his son about the brother he had never seen; the boy who had been born in Poland after Howard had left. The boy who somehow escaped the Holocaust and turned up in Buenos Aires wrote Howard a letter in 1947; then he neither answered any letters from his brother nor contacted the Silvers family in any other way, until a brief letter arrived in 1985, four months after Howard Silvers' death.

Ira, the male heir, answered at once. And to nobody's surprise, the junior Silvers also received no response until the note in February 1987, from a Señor Cardozo, informing Ira that his uncle had died in 1986.

Ira felt no grief when he read the news. How could he mourn an abstraction, an uncle who was less real to him than other family exotica, the tablecloth from Shanghai or the tea service from Budapest, historical items that came out on special occasions? Carlos stayed hidden. A name, a South American. "Maybe a gangster," Ira's mother guessed.

If Howard Silvers had an opinion about the fate of his unknown brother, he never told it to his son. When it came to immigrant tales Howard preferred his own, and Ira didn't blame him.

The Howard Silvers saga had no Nazi terror or Jewish blood. The adventure of a happy-go-lucky boy who takes on the world, to Ira, was like Robin Hood, only this one starred Howard Silvers. Ira could still hear it in his father's intonation.

"I was born with a smell for the big world," Howard Silvers would say. "I had an American soul, but in my village there were only two things: study and pray. Study, study, study, then pray, pray, pray. It was making me crazy. When I was thirteen and they said I was a man, I made up my mind to act like one. The next time one of those black-bearded teachers hit me I told myself that would be it, and it was. I ran away. But don't think I was thirteen the way American boys are thirteen. I *was* a man. I passed for seventeen and got a job on a merchant ship. I shoveled coal across the Atlantic. I had muscles like this."

"It's true," Harriet Silvers would interrupt. "Your father was as strong as a horse."

Ira's mother, Harriet, a third-generation native of Savannah, Georgia, raised her son as heir to the Old South rather than the Old World.

"By the time I met him," Harriet would say, "your father had no accent and was already an accountant. I didn't believe it when he told me he had run away from Poland in 1929. He was a self-made man. I fell in love."

While Howard Silvers established himself in Richmond, Virginia, Carlos of Buenos Aires sank into obscurity, became a name.

To Ira, growing up in Richmond, Buenos Aires meant Uncle Carlos the way Texas meant oil or Africa meant lions.

Then, in the mid-1950s, after eight years of unanswered letters, Howard Silvers gave up contacting Carlos.

"If he wants a brother, he knows where to find one," the accountant said, and that was it, until 1986.

Ira, looking for clues to his lost uncle, had only one. The letter announcing Carlos's death was signed by Señor Elisha Cardozo, and it carried a return address.

Silvers telephoned, then took the number 11 bus as directed in his pocket guide to Buenos Aires. The pocket guide also informed Ira that he was heading toward the Buenos Aires garment center, "similar to New York's Seventh Avenue," the pamphlet said, but when Silvers got off the bus and walked away from the Avenida Corrientes, the expensive luggage and shoe stores disappeared and he saw twisted streets full of shops featuring yard goods, fabrics, notions, liners—crowded nineteenth-century facades that reminded him of the Lower East Side.

He found the address, number 97 on Calle Larrea, a wooden gate between a store of curtain hooks and an emporium of mothballs and Velcro.

Until the woman came to the gate to admit him, Silvers did not know there was a Señora Cardozo.

The elderly lady led him to her apartment through a small courtyard half in bloom. Next to a banana palm, Silvers saw the open shower and what he guessed was the shared toilet. At the rear of the courtyard Señora Cardozo welcomed him to her three tiny rooms.

"It is I," she said, "who wrote you the letter. I speak the king's English."

Already awaiting the American on her mahogany dining-room table were tea, date cookies, and, ubiquitous in Buenos Aires, a plate of sliced beef.

Señora Cardozo welcomed Ira as a guest, but Silvers, too curious to be polite, asked what she knew about his uncle even before he sipped his tea.

Señora Cardozo unfortunately had scant information.

"Maybe I saw him in the synagogue," she said, "maybe not. My husband, he will tell you."

Señor Cardozo, she said, was expected at any moment.

While they waited, Señora Cardozo wanted to show the American a few things. From a bookcase she pulled down her albums. Expecting grandchildren, Silvers was surprised to see women in evening gowns. He thought Señora Cardozo was showing him a photo album of an old Miss Buenos Aires pageant.

"All mine," the señora said.

"Daughters?"

"No"—she laughed—"the gowns. My life's work. Since I was eight years old my mother taught me dressmaking, in England, before I came here."

She held up her right hand, then, as if an afterthought, her left. "Who knows how many dresses these fingers have made?"

Señora Cardozo began to narrate her way through the smiling women in prom gowns.

Silvers looked at his watch.

"This one you will know," she said.

Silvers shook his head.

"Gisela Glandt."

She skipped a few laminated pages and pointed to a woman holding a microphone desperately, as if it were a life raft.

"Her you will know from the radio all over the world."

"I'm not up on radio," Silvers said.

He had had his fill of beehive hairdos, plump smiles, and 1950s gowns. He didn't want to be rude, but he closed the album and moved it from his lap to the table.

"Some of the girls," Señora Cardozo said, "are not girls anymore. Some have already left this life. But the dresses they passed on to their daughters. My work lasts."

To distract her from opening the second album, Silvers told her about his own work.

Señora Cardozo immediately offered her services to the film industry.

Silvers told her that the film he was working on was science fiction.

"They don't need gowns," he said. "The characters aren't human."

"Still," the dressmaker said, "there must be females and formal occasions."

She opened the second album, looking for Helena Ferranto, an actress. Silvers decided he had seen enough.

"I have to get back to the set," he said. "I'll call your husband tonight."

He was already planning to meet her husband in a café.

"No, no, no," Señora Cardozo said. She blocked the doorway with her bony self.

"Señor Cardozo will not forgive me if he doesn't see you."

When Silvers had moved back to his seat, the señora, moving as quickly as a child, went to the bedroom. Silvers heard her excited voice on the telephone. When she opened the door he spotted, above the unmade bed, a crucifix.

"Cardozo will be here faster than a pig can eat," she said, proud of her colloquialism.

Silvers wondered about the crucifix but decided it was none of his business.

An hour later, after he had finished the platter of meat and all the cookies and had looked through the second album, Silvers told the señora that he absolutely could wait no longer.

"I'm late. People are waiting."

She blocked the door again, but this time Silvers was prepared if necessary to move her aside.

"Five more minutes," she pleaded. "It will be worth it, you'll see."

The door opened, and above the old woman's head Silvers looked into the eyes of a movie star.

"Nora Cortez," she called herself, "an actress."

Silvers could not look away. With twilight and the dingy courtyard as backdrop, Nora modeled a gown that only Señora Cardozo could have made. The red material dipped into the young woman's chest, made a sliver of her waist, then blossomed into a garden of flowers that wilted at her ankles.

Nora, perhaps a model as well as an actress, did not mind being looked at. Without posing or becoming embarrassed, she accepted Silvers' stare and seemed equally intent on looking at him.

Señora Cardozo stood between them. When she was sure of the writer's interest, she taunted him.

"Mr. Silvers is late," she told Nora. "He has to leave."

Silvers no longer noticed her. The three of them stood in the doorway for a few seconds, then the old lady, satisfied, went into the kitchen.

Silvers walked with Nora through the crowded streets of the garment district. Workers, on their way home, stepped aside for the beautiful woman in the hooped skirt. Nora was embarrassed.

"Señora Cardozo insisted that I wear this," she said. "Please forgive me. I did not want to disappoint her."

"If I knew where to rent a tuxedo around here," Ira said, "I would do it, and we could go to the opera or something."

"I've never been to an opera," Nora said.

"Neither have I," Silvers told the truth. "I was just trying to sound impressive."

When Silvers invited her to dinner, Nora gave him the address of a restaurant and went home to change. He offered to take her home by cab, but Nora insisted on going home alone and on foot.

Silvers watched her disappear among the bookstalls on Avenida de Corrientes. When she turned the corner, he had a terrible premonition that he would never see her again. He waited for a minute, trying to act rational; then he attempted to follow her, but when he came to the crosswalk there were only pedestrians on the sidewalk, no Cinderellas, no dark-eyed Spanish beauties who'd just stepped out of eighteenth-century paintings.

At the Parilla Restaurant, which he quickly located, Silvers drank a salty beer as he awaited Nora. He tried to remain calm. In the men's room he washed his face and ran wet fingers through his curly hair. He wanted to look good for her even though he had resigned himself to believing she would not come to the restaurant.

If this happened, he would return to the Cardozo apartment and find Nora on one of the album pages. On the back he would read her biographical facts, her statistics, or if not, the old dressmaker would give Silvers her phone number.

Then, on time, actually ten minutes early, Nora appeared. Though she now wore blue jeans and a man-tailored shirt, she still looked to Silvers as if she could perch on a museum wall.

She laughed when he told her how worried he had been.

"Señora Cardozo told me you could help me find a film role. She convinced me that I had to appear in costume. I was so ashamed. I felt like—what you call her—Scarlett O'Hara."

"You could be a movie star," Silvers said. He could hardly believe such a cliché could come from him. It was a phrase his mother used. "I mean, you certainly have what it takes."

"What it takes," Nora said, "is an opportunity, no?"

Silvers knew what she wanted and felt his insignificance in Feldman's project. Briefly he imagined going to the producer with new scenes, a new character, Nora, the Queen of Baltimore, riding along the waterfront on a barge like Cleopatra entering Rome.

"I wish I could help," he said, "but it's already cast. Anyway, you would not want to be in this film." He was embarrassed as he told her the plot.

"It's about microscopic creatures from another planet who land at the Baltimore County Sewage plant. To them human waste is paradise. It's the ultimate power source, what nuclear fusion would be to us. They use one day's worth of Baltimore sewage to take over the world. The producer thinks it's so disgusting that it will become a cult classic."

Silvers was smiling an embarrassed smile, but the actress looked intent, as if he had narrated to her the plot of *The Brothers Karamazov.*

"I have heard of Feldman," she said. "He makes many films."

"Don't judge me by him," Ira said. "I hardly know the man."

"But you work for him."

"Yes, maybe for a few weeks."

Silvers wanted to move the conversation away from business.

"Let's make a deal: you won't connect me with Feldman and I won't connect you with Señora Cardozo."

"Without the señora," Nora said, "we would not know each other."

Silvers raised his glass. "To Señora Cardozo in gratitude."

They drank several more toasts to the señora, and one sweet one to their new friendship, but once the food arrived, the evening took an awkward turn. Silvers, unaccustomed even in the States to dripping barbecue sauce, needed a dozen napkins to dab at his lips. He was embarrassed and felt that he seemed coarse to this Argentinian beauty who could hold a sticky rib with her fingertips and gnaw at it the way a cat might, hardly disturbing the flesh, making it melt toward a blackened bone.

He was so busy with chewing and wiping his lips that he felt unable to charm or even interest her. He needed to count on the lure of his connection to the movies. For their next date he was already planning a café setting. They would order small, clean pastries and white wine.

He did learn that Nora was twenty-two and had been taking acting classes. By day she worked as a typist in an insurance office. Recently she had given up the classes because they were too expensive. She was looking for a second job in the evenings.

"The inflation," she said, "it makes people crazy. You think there is never enough of anything, and it's true."

She also wanted to improve her English.

After dinner, Nora arose, shook Silvers' hand, and said goodbye.

"Wait," he said. "I'll take you home. I would love to help you with your English."

Silvers had been imagining a few drinks, maybe even, depending on the situation and of course, her attitude, an invitation to the Hotel Grand Plaza. She was already out the door before Silvers, leaving a wad of cash on the table, rushed from the restaurant to catch her. She gave him her phone number but refused his plea to walk her home. Still, as she handed him the slip of paper with her number, Nora kissed his cheekbone before she disappeared among the early evening shoppers.

Nobody answered at the phone number she gave him. Silvers tried all day, until midnight. After that hour, he thought, it's not my business.

The day after that when she didn't answer, he couldn't stand it and returned to the Cardozo apartment.

This time the gentleman himself awaited Silvers. He was a dapper man, in his seventies, with a trim white mustache and a silk cravat such as Silvers had seen worn only by characters in films.

Señor Cardozo bowed at the waist to his guest. It only took a few minutes for Silvers to realize that his host modeled himself on Douglas Fairbanks Jr.

Though still curious, of course, about his uncle, Silvers wanted information about the living, about Nora.

The dapper gentleman ignored Silvers' straightforward request for Nora's work number. He looked at the ceiling of his squalid apartment, held his hand to his heart, and seemed to be fighting off painful memory.

"I hardly knew the man," Cardozo said. "He came to the synagogue on high holy days only. I'm not much better. You know how it is, one forgets the old ways."

Recalling the crucifix in the Cardozo bedroom, Ira suspected just how much forgetting there had been.

"I regret," Cardozo said, "that I don't even know his last name. I only knew him as Carlos."

With shame, Silvers admitted he was not certain.

"Our name is Silvers. In Poland it was Slavititsky. I don't know what name Carlos went by here. I addressed the letter that your wife answered to Carlos Silvers, care of this address. It was the address he used."

"Of course," Carlos said. "So that my wife could read him the English. I do know that he was a modest man. He prayed in a corner of the synagogue. I believe he worked on a loading dock. He was a strong man. Arms like this."

Suddenly, in this detail, Silvers for the first time recognized his uncle. Carlos became a man, like Howard the sailor, or Howard the father who had entertained his little son by making his huge biceps jump. Ira himself had none of the Silvers' arm strength. Tall and thin as a Virginia elm, he resembled the delicate Georgians, his mother's relatives.

"How did your wife happen to write the letter in English to me?" Ira asked.

"Carlos brought your English letter to us to translate. He was very sad to learn that his brother was dead. I offered to write for him, but he said not now. He left your letter here, so naturally when we heard he was dead, she wrote to you."

Finally the aged fop turned his mournful look to use. "You could give a donation to the synagogue in his memory," he said. "It would be very helpful."

"I'm not a rich man," Silvers said. "This movie job is a rare experience for me."

Silvers asked again about Nora Cortez.

"Yes, yes, Nora," Cardozo said, "a true beauty."

Before he said anything else about Nora, Cardozo extracted a promise from Ira to visit the synagogue on Friday night.

"There's no rabbi, no cantor," he said, "just a group of old men. We used to be a burial society. Now it's more like a religious club. You'll visit, you'll sip a little wine, then you'll decide about a donation."

For the third time the writer asked for Nora's number at the insurance office. The old man gave him the same phone number he already had.

"That's all there is," Cardozo swore. "Even my wife has no other number."

The señora, of course, was not at home.

"Fitting a gown for a circus performer," Cardozo said, although Ira was certain he heard her whispering to her husband when Cardozo went into the bedroom for the phone number.

Though he knew it was hopeless, Silvers looked for Nora on the streets. He spent two whole days at outdoor cafés on the Ricoletto. He sipped coffee after coffee and went, on the half hour, to use the men's room and the telephone. Waiters began to recognize him. Nora did not answer.

At a bookstall he bought an English grammar, a gift for Nora, so she would know how genuinely he wanted to help her with her English.

Surrounded by verbs, Silvers' lonely imagination raced. He would invite her to America, help her find a typing job in Baltimore. He would do this out of disinterested friendship, asking nothing in return.

Still Silvers, breathing in the cigarette smoke of the Buenos Aires literati as he read his English grammar in a café beside the carved tomb of Eva Perón, dreamed a man's dreams. Wearing the red dress, Nora came to his apartment on Charles Street. She carried a tiny suitcase like a stewardess. At first she was shy. Then she kissed his cheek and whispered in his ear. And soon his bony American knee pressed against the roses of her red gown.

At the surrounding tables couples whispered, talked with their hands, blew dark smoke to heaven. Silvers could stand it no longer.

Breaking into a jog as he left the street of cafes, he ran toward the Jewish Federation Building. If he could not find the living, he would divert himself among the dead.

This was no easy job. The officials of the new three-story building a few blocks from the Cardozos' apartment were not sympathetic. He was seeking an uncle, dead for two years, whose last name he did not know. For that matter even Carlos might have been a nom de plume. All Silvers really had was the date of death, and that was accurate only within months, in the summer of 1986. In spring the Cardozos had seen Carlos, but by the high holy days he was no more.

Finally, after being shunted from office to office, Silvers sat alone in the basement of the Organización de Judios de Buenos Aires reading alphabetically the 1986 list of Jewish dead.

Under Silvers he found four entries, even one about the right age: Emanuel, but this departed Silvers had been born in Buenos Aires and had left a half-column list of survivors, hardly the thick-muscled Polish-born dockworker that Cardozo described as his uncle.

Under Slavititsky he found no listing. There were no other reasonable possibilities, but because Ira had nothing better to do, he read through the entire list of 1986 Jewish dead. None could have been his uncle Carlos.

When he returned the volumes that looked like the ledger books in his father's office in the precomputer days, the clerk told him there was only one other possibility.

"If your uncle had nobody, he might have been buried by the gentiles at the public cemetery."

"Would they bury a Jew there?"

"This is a big city," the clerk said. "If there's a corpse and nobody claims it, the authorities bury it. Jew, gentile, whatever."

"But would there be a record?"

"Of course," the clerk said. "This is not a primitive country."

"I'm surprised," Silvers said, "that the Jewish community has no record of a man who lived in Buenos Aires for at least forty years."

"The Jewish community," the clerk reminded the American, "relies on names. We are not magicians."

On Friday morning, Silvers, still in bed, heard from Feldman. The producer, calling from Santiago de Chile, had canceled the production. Instead of Silvers' script, he was going to remain in Chile to shoot a vampire movie.

"I'm sorry," Feldman said. "Still, you got a week below the equator out of this, and you learned something. Never trust the unions. They're all Communists."

The producer had managed to get Silvers a seat to Miami on Sunday even though the Argentinian airline was on strike.

"You're going on AeroPeru. Let's keep in touch."

The end of his film-writing career was no disappointment. Silvers even felt relief that he would not have to see Feldman again, but how could he leave without seeing Nora?

On Friday evening as he promised, Silvers went to services in the company of Señor Cardozo. The gentleman appeared even more dapper in his linen suit plus cravat. Silvers, a Reform Jew who went to temple on the high holidays when he remembered, had no idea what to expect from Cardozo's congregation.

He suspected there would be old men passing around Torahs wrapped in dark velveteen. He would not have been surprised by incense or stirring harangues in Hebrew or Yiddish, languages obsolete and meaningless to him.

No matter what, in advance Silvers had made a policy decision. He would make a donation in his uncle's memory but only fifty dollars, not a penny more. To a live uncle he would have been generous, but for the nameless dead he set a fifty-dollar limit. Like his father before him, for cash Silvers wanted results. To the Cardozos he owed nothing at all, especially since neither the aged señor nor his wife gave him any information about Nora.

Silvers, without any options left, played his last card.

"It's too bad about Nora," he told Señor Cardozo. "I've tried to phone her. There is a part, but if she doesn't reach me by tomorrow it will be too late. A shame. I did everything I could. I'll be in my hotel right after services."

In the synagogue, actually a room in an old house with a dining-room table and some folding chairs, Silvers prayed for a message from Nora. He knew it was crazy, but he said his prayer like a mantra: "Call me, call me, call me." When he stopped chanting to himself he wondered what he would do if she called. What if she even fulfilled his fantasies and slept with him? So what? He would be back in Baltimore and she would remain in Buenos Aires, typing to fight off inflation. His romance, like his film script, was a stillbirth. No *Filth*, no love, not even information on his uncle. His week in Buenos Aires amounted to three strikes, even worse. He now dreaded going back to his solitary life in Baltimore, feared that his old defenses against solitude would no longer help. In this makeshift synagogue among fewer than ten old men, Silvers, without moving his lips, repeated Nora's name in rhythm to the Spanish songs around him.

"It's a friendship society, even more than a synagogue," Cardozo told him.

"Did my uncle come often?"

"No," Cardozo said, "just on the holidays. He had his own book."

A new fact. Late in the game, Silvers discovered that Carlos owned a Hebrew book.

"Would the book be here?"

Cardozo shook his head.

After the service one of the congregants shook Silvers' hand, spoke in English, and gave him a gift, a small red Gideon Bible. Silvers was no stranger to the book. Such Bibles were regularly given to children in Virginia, but by Christian missionaries, not by Jews.

Silvers dropped the book into the pocket of his blazer, as useful to him as a ticket stub.

Cardozo watched the transaction and looked embarrassed.

"What kind of synagogue is this?" Silvers asked his host as they walked out together. "That man gave me a Christian Bible."

"It is all one God," Cardozo said. "The Christians come, you tell them fine. Jesus was a good man. Things stay peaceful."

"You've got a cross in your house," Silvers blurted out. "What kind of a Jew are you?"

Silvers' passion surprised him. He pulled the Gideon Bible out of his pocket and handed it to Cardozo.

"I don't believe my uncle was part of your congregation," Silvers said.

"On high holidays," Cardozo said, "it's all Jews. Then we pray in the old ways. The rest of the year, who cares? You go out for a little company."

In the sweaty palm of his right hand Silvers clutched a fifty-dollar bill.

"I'll give you a donation," Silvers said, "but only if I can see Nora. No lies, no excuses."

The elegant gentleman pulled a watch out of the pocket of his trousers, snapped it open.

"I know my wife," he said. "Nora has already called you." Silvers gave him the fifty, then ran as fast as he could through the crowded streets toward the Avenida de Corrientes, where the cabs on Friday night were plentiful.

When he got to the hotel Nora sat on a flowered couch in the lobby waiting. She was wearing a gray jersey dress. Her eyes were swollen.

Silvers, a madman, ran to her.

"I've called you every half hour for days," he yelled.

People in the lobby looked at him. Silvers didn't care. Nora stood. Silvers pressed her against him.

"I love you," he said.

"I know," she said. "I heard the phone ring."

In his arms she sobbed and let him kiss her. He led her toward the elevators.

In his room Silvers, a starving man, kissed her ears, her cheeks, her eyes. Her tears wet the back of his neck.

"I lied," he said. "There's no part, no film. I just had to see you. I've been losing my mind."

Nora did not resist him. He buried his face in her neck. He kissed the soft tops of her breasts, drew her waist to him as a lover.

"No," Nora said, "we cannot. There are things you do not understand."

She moved away from Silvers, straightened her dress.

"I wanted to tell you right away but I could not."

She closed her eyes, then said it. "I can avoid it no longer. I am your uncle's daughter."

That night Silvers learned some of the facts.

"My mother is a Christian," Nora said. "My father lived like us. Only once a year he went among the Jews. We knew he had a brother in America, but he made us promise never to tell."

With Nora's help Silvers located his uncle. Nora led, and Silvers carried the flashlight. As he stood beside Carlos, a tiny hump beneath a cross, Silvers grieved for his father's baby brother. Tears of love and sorrow fell from his eyes, and from his cousin's.

"Now I've told," Nora said. "Forgive me, Father."

She encircled Ira in her strong Silvers arms. His lips on Nora's wet cheeks, his heart as confused as it was aroused, Ira mourned his uncle and foresaw himself surrounded by family.

House of the Lowered

AS SOON AS he heard that Carlos was coming to visit him before the 92nd shipped out to Iraq, Elario decided to throw a party. "Barbecue, mariachi, the works," he said. "The marine is landing in Houston." Though he rarely saw his son, Elario talked about him a lot. "Carlos always knew he had a father," he told me, "it wasn't much, sometimes maybe ten dollars a month, but every day of his life that boy knew he had a father who sent money."

I had to hand it to Elario, he'd come a long way. Two years ago, when he asked for credit, I didn't even know his name, but I recognized him because he'd been coming in for a few weeks to window shop double quad speakers.

"Mr. Aaron," he said, "el diablo needs sound, some blocks, and a skirt."

"You're talking close to a thousand," I said.

"I'm gonna give you this," he said, "for collateral."

He put into my hand a head shot of a teenage boy in a little frame that he pulled right off his keychain.

"Is this an antique or something?" I asked.

"That's Carlos," he said, "he's on the track team at San Antonio Union." I looked at it and I thought, this guy is not a good credit risk.

"Every weekend I'll work the money off," he said, "trees, lawns, plumbing, whatever you need."

I did have a lot of yard work so even though I knew better, I jacked up the price by 25 percent and gave him the credit. The next Saturday Elario showed up at my house in a '57 Chevy that I didn't think would ever make it out of the driveway. He'd lowered that Bel-Air coupe to maybe three inches over the road.

"You're risking your chrome on every pothole," I warned him.

"You're right," he said, "but what can I do? The snake loves it." He pointed to the reptile on his left arm. I saw that particular tattoo on lots of gang members and in various colors. Elario had the long model, shoulder all the way to his wrist with the snake's head on the back of his hand. "Who's running the show?" I asked him, "you or the snake?" He laughed about that the whole time he worked on my flowerbeds.

In a hundred years I would never have thought that someone like Elario would end up in the store, but when I put out the Help Wanted sign he had already worked off his credit so I gave him a shot at the job. Maybe he has cost me a few sales because of those gold chains and his partly chewed off ear, but most of our customers come from the barrio, and, like I told him, I believe that by all rights Houston should still be part of Mexico.

He disagreed. The Mexican cops were worse, he said. Everyone was on the take and the judges were all whores. At least in Houston after a few days you could make a decent bail arrangement. But that was all in his past. I trust Elario every day with the cash register and a lot more.

When I needed help with Mom, Elario was the one who came through. He brought over his own mother, Luisa, from somewhere near Oaxaca. He took five days off work; drove down there and then snuck her over the border. Don't ask–don't tell is my policy, too.

"She's strong and clean," he said, "she can carry a sofa on her back, I've seen her do that, but back home she can't earn a dollar an hour." I had had it with one agency hire after another not showing up to take care of my mother, who has Alzheimer's but is okay below the neck. She just can't be left alone. And some of those so-called caregivers are worse than alone. Mom would need an IV before they'd get off their butt to give her a drink.

So, our mothers live together and everyone is happy. Sure, Luisa is probably bored, but every couple of days she rearranges the furniture and they always walk down to the thrift stores and to Safeway.

"It's better than she had in Oaxaca," Elario says. He doesn't visit his mother much, but when he does and his eight speakers blast, Luisa thinks her son is a cruise missile coming down I-45. And she loves to wash his thick whitewalls with the counterspin hubcaps.

I can talk to Luisa because my Spanish is good in the present tense. Mom doesn't understand a word, but it's just as well. Luisa makes signs to her and squeals and laughs and Mom seems to like it. Once they leave the apartment, Luisa never lets go of Mom's hand. She's only about five feet tall, but she's got big arms and carries close to two hundred pounds.

When Carlos called to say that he was coming to say good-bye to his dad before he shipped out, Elario got all sappy. "When he was born, I told Marta we should name him Holiday Inn. Whenever she knew there was going to be an early checkout on her floor she'd call me and say, 'can you be here in ten minutes?' I was always there in five—I was only seventeen."

Elario asked me if he could use the store parking lot for the barbecue because he had no room at his apartment. "I'd be honored," I said, and I meant it. I was looking forward to meeting Carlos, the marine.

"After he was born," Elario said, "I thought, Jesus, I'm gonna have fifty kids before I'm through, but you know what, he's the only one."

"You're not exactly out of business yet," I said.

"Everything is in the hand of God," he said.

And I sure found out how true that is when a guy who was talking on his cell phone rammed the side of my Chrysler going at least forty. I lucked out in the accident, just broken ribs and a ruptured spleen in a totaled Chrysler. When I healed up, I decided that I would do something to help others. I called Temple Beth Israel to volunteer. I don't go much but I've been a member all my life. The temple has a committee for just about everything—overweight teens, mourners, singles under forty, over forty, interfaith, outreach—I narrowed it down to visiting the sick or temple maintenance, and finally, I chose the sick over something like stacking chairs in the audiovisual room.

After I sent in the paperwork, I got a welcoming call from assistant Rabbi Epstein. The office kept a list of sick members updated daily, but he warned me to call first before going to visit a hospital because they don't hold people like they used to. That I already knew. I didn't tell him about my own hospitalization because I hadn't listed any religious preference and I felt a little embarrassed by that when talking to a rabbi.

The first sick person that the temple assigned to me was Morris Fisher. The rabbi said he didn't know the man but he was in room 808 at Methodist Hospital. Methodist, I've heard, is where the King of Saudi Arabia stays when he comes to Texas. They keep a section of one floor roped off for whenever he decides to use it, and for that kind of service the king drops a few million a year on the hospital. Maybe it's not true.

Anyway, Mr. Fisher was in a regular room and when I knocked and then came in he was half sitting up in bed, the game of solitaire laid across his lap. He looked about seventy-five and there were no tubes sticking out of him. I didn't know why he was in the hospital. He held part of the deck in his hand. He didn't even say hello, he just stared at me for a while, then he asked me to repeat my name. "Aaron Evans," I said, and I gave him one of my business cards. "When you're feeling better, stop by if you like auto accessories." His legs twitched and there went his solitaire game all over the floor.

"Don't worry, I'll get the cards," I said, "it's been a while since I've seen anyone playing real solitaire now that every cell phone has the electronic version." While I squatted under his bed I explained that I was from the temple visiting committee.

"I didn't think it would be like this," he said, "I thought you would sneak in."

"I don't know what the rules are for the visiting committee," I said, "but why would I want to sneak in?"

I was already wishing that I had picked temple maintenance even before he asked, "Are you allowed to talk about your mission?"

"We can talk about anything you want, "I said, "baseball, cars, politics . . ." He shook his head. "I understand why you're here," he said, "maybe in the days of the Torah, visitors like you talked about sheep and goats."

I began to wonder if Mr. Fisher was a mental case even though Methodist isn't that kind of hospital. I told him again who I was and why I was visiting him.

"Beth Israel," he repeated the name of the temple slowly, as if he was recalling it. "You've come to me from the house of Israel. That's good. He knows that I haven't always wanted to be there, but that's where I belong now."

I was glad to see him perking up a little.

"House of Israel," he said, "talk to me about the end of days, your specialty."

"My specialty," I told him, "is cars, what you probably call hot rods, you know, trim, special lowering kits, things like that. Modification."

"I've been ready since my wife died; we don't have to wait."

I was getting pretty uncomfortable, so I just asked him if we could watch TV and he said that was okay. I turned on the Astros game and made a few comments about Roger Clemens, who was pitching, and I thought that if Mr. Fisher stopped talking nonsense, I might stay for an entire inning. And it seemed like he was watching the game, too, until he said, "Let's not beat around the bush anymore, take me with you now and save everyone a lot of trouble."

I heard a nurse walking down the hall and as soon as she came in and strapped a blood pressure cuff on him, I shook his hand and said I had to go. He didn't let go of my hand.

"Do you know the date?" he asked.

"It's June sixth," I said, "I know it because it's D-Day."

"Do you have to visit again?" he asked.

"I could if you want me to," I said.

"It won't be necessary," he said, then he let go of my hand and I got out of there.

I pretty much knew what Mr. Fisher was getting at and that soured me on hospital visiting. I decided that in the future I would do my good deeds in some other, more cheerful way, maybe something with children.

I didn't forget about Fisher, I just decided not to think about what might have happened to him. Then, a month or so later, a man dressed in a suit and tie, which is unusual for our store, came in and asked for me. "He's a Fed or a collector," Elario said. Jacob Fisher was about forty, my own age, round faced with a fleshy nose. He gave me his card, a lawyer in some downtown office.

"I don't know if you remember visiting my father," he said.

I said that I remembered and right away I worried that maybe he'd come to sue me about something. I was trying to recall if I had actually touched his father and I was pretty sure that I hadn't laid a hand on the man except to shake hello and good-bye. "How's your dad?" I asked but I figured that the old gentleman was long gone.

"His health is good, in fact excellent," Jacob Fisher said, "although he doesn't believe it. He thinks that he has only a short time to live. In his mind he's made some kind of arrangement with God, and you, Aaron Evans, are the messenger of doom, the stranger sent to him by God Almighty."

Elario, who was listening, loved this. "Tell your papa that he's got the wrong man," Elario said. "El diablo has the skull and crossbones seat covers and the antenna with the pirate flag."

Jacob Fisher looked at me as if calling for translation. "El diablo is his car," I said, "the skulls, the snake, it's gang stuff. Most of them are really not bad guys, I do a lot of business with gangs. For them, Mr. Death is just their favorite dress-up game; for some of them every day is Halloween."

"If we could get back to my father's situation," he said.

"I didn't bring up any of this with your dad," I said. "I just came in to say hello from temple."

"I understand," Jacob Fisher said, "Dad's surgery was 100 percent successful. He's seventy-three, not so old these days."

I agreed.

"But he has given up on life, he's ready to go. His house is all packed and labeled; he sold his car. He's a widower, my mother died four years ago. He says that September sixth is his date, exactly three months from the day of your visit."

"Well, on September seventh his worries should be over," I said, "one way or another."

"I'm not able to joke about it," Jacob Fisher said. "The psychiatrist and I are afraid that he really might make it happen, the mind is a powerful thing—and I even worry about, God forbid, suicide."

I could see what a big thing this was for the son, and I sympathized because I know what it's like to have a parent who's in outer space.

"The reason that I'm here," he said, "is to ask your permission to bring Dad for a visit to you. Maybe seeing that you own a store and are just a person will help him to snap out of it. The psychiatrist agrees that it's a good idea."

"It's okay with me," I said.

"I have offered to take Dad to Florida, to Israel, anywhere. His answer is always the same, 'You can't escape Aaron Evans.'"

Elario burst out laughing. "I love it," he said, "we should print that on a bumper sticker." He made his voice creepy like a television commercial for a horror movie, "You can't escape Aaron Evans."

"Cut it," I said, "this isn't about playing tough guy in the neighborhood. Mr. Fisher believes that God sent me to him."

"The drugos all believe that, too," Elario said. "I've seen guys in church so flooded that they can't stand up, but ask them about God and they'll tell you that they're the bleeding heart."

"Forget it," I said. I walked Jacob Fisher to his car, a dark blue Jaguar. I didn't even stock anything for a car like that, and I apologized for Elario. After meeting his son, that's when I really started to think a lot about Mr. Fisher. I didn't feel responsible for him but his situation bothered me enough to call Rabbi Epstein, whom I shake hands with at high holidays, but I don't really know. I told him about my visit and asked about the angel of death stuff. I wanted to know if it was a Jewish thing.

"It's all superstition," he said, "there is no such character in Judaism. Of course there are stories. In every culture people personify death. When there's the unknowable or a man carrying a scythe and wearing a black hood, we prefer what we can see." He said that neither Morris Fisher nor his son had called him, but he would check in with them to see if he could be of any help. The rabbi wasn't surprised either, he had heard of such situations before. "Sometimes just being in the hospital brings on these encounters with mortality," he said. He advised me to forget about it, and maybe I would have if Elario hadn't started calling me Señor Muerte. Finally, I had to tell him that if he didn't stop, I would cancel the Carlos party, which I began to think might never happen because we hadn't heard from him again. Then he called one Thursday, to say he'd be in on Sunday to say good-bye. With so little notice we had to hurry to get the party arranged. We have regular store hours, noon to seven on Sunday, so I posted a sign "closing at 4 Sunday," and I called a mariachi band and ordered eight cases of beer and lots of barbecue and hot dogs. I told Elario that I would cover the expenses. "How many times am I going to have a chance to do something for a marine?" I said.

Just before the barbecue, I finally met Carlos. He was a skinny kid, maybe 130 and about five foot ten. I had expected a big hulking marine, more like Elario, who has a cannon-sized beer gut, and Luisa, who is a pure block. "A small mother," I thought.

I told Carlos to pick anything he wanted from the shop to decorate his tank or Humvee or whatever the marines used for transport, but all he picked was a set of mud flaps for a Honda. Then the barbecue problem came up. "I've been a vegetarian," Carlos said. "I started eating meat in basic because I had to, but I was thinking that this weekend, while I'm off, I'd like to get by on veggies."

"You hear that," Elario said, "he eats meat for his country. When did you start this vegetarian crap?"

"When I was a junior in high school," Carlos said, "didn't I ever tell you? Don't worry about it, I can buy a pack of veggie dogs, there's all kinds of them."

"You'll buy nothing," Elario said, "this is my party for you. French fries are okay though?"

"Perfect," Carlos said.

Elario had invited his buddies from the gang days, although I don't think he traveled with them that much anymore.

I closed the store at 3:30 to give Elario time to set up, then I went out to pick up supplies and later, Luisa and Mom. When I got there the two of them were in a tug of war over Mom's thermal jacket. Luisa was trying to pull it off her. "You're right," I told Luisa, "it's 92, but if she wants to wear a jacket, don't fight her." In the lobby, Mom zipped her jacket as if to prove that she was right. Luisa had painted Mom's fingernails bright red, and hers, too. She was excited about seeing her grandson Carlos, whom she had never met. She already had a grandson named Carlos in Oaxaca, but that Carlos was just a baby.

I pulled up at the store with the ladies about 5:30. The fire was already going and there were a lot of people I recognized from the neighborhood. Then I spotted Morris Fisher and his son Jacob mingling in the crowd, each of them holding a longneck. The old man was wearing a tallit. I didn't mind him being there even if he thought it was a bar mitzvah, I just didn't want the old guy to go ballistic when he spotted me.

Luisa gave Carlos a bone-crushing hug, only he wasn't Carlos. She had grabbed one of Elario's buddies and lifted him into the air. When she put him down he did the same to her. Carlos was over by the steel drum barbecue watching his veggie dogs to make sure they didn't get mixed in with the other ones. He wasn't in uniform so I couldn't blame Luisa for not knowing which one was her grandson.

"Hi there," I said to Fisher and his son, "enjoy the party."

"Do you see?" Jacob said to his father, "It's all in your imagination. Aaron is a man, just like everyone else. He owns this store. You're standing in his parking lot." I gave the thumbs up to that.

Morris Fisher pointed to mom. "He's dragging the old lady away. Her time has come."

"She's my mother," I said, but it did look like I was dragging her along.

"September sixth," he said, "then it will be my turn."

"Stop it, dad!" Jacob Fisher said. "This is a party, don't spoil it for Aaron."

He pointed to Mom again. "She shouldn't be at a party, her party days are over."

Elario had finally gotten Luisa to the right person, and she was hugging and picking up her grandson.

"Look at that," Elario called out to me. "Isn't that beautiful? The marine and his grandma. Does anyone give a fuck if she's got a green card?"

Elario raised a longneck to make a toast. "For Carlos," he sang out, "my son the marine. Stay safe and kick some ass over there."

Everybody cheered.

Carlos stood up on the bench and said, "Thanks, dad, and thank you everyone, but we're not going over there to kick ass. We're peacemakers, that's what marines are all about."

Hector, one of Elario's buddies who came to the store now and then, grabbed Carlos from behind in a playful headlock. Like most of the men, Hector wore a leather vest over his bare chest, and he rubbed the marine's face against his graying chest hairs and the ornamental crosses that hung from his neck. “I’m a peacemaker, too,” he yelled, “get me into some action.”

When the mariachi band started playing, Hector released the marine and Carlos took his grandmother by the hand and we all made a circle around them. Luisa could really dance. It surprised me how light on her feet she was. I wanted her to stay beside Mom so that I could circulate but I didn’t want to spoil her fun so I got mom a barbecue and settled her into a chair and made sure that she had a big wad of napkins.

“You okay?” I asked her.

“I’m hungry,” she said.

I pointed to the sandwich right in front of her. “Eat,” I said.

There were about forty or fifty people on the parking lot and a couple of good-looking women, but they were too fat, and anyway I wasn’t about to strike up a conversation with someone else’s woman, not in this crowd. When I had a chance, I moved over to say a few words to the marine.

“You can’t be too careful over there,” I said.

“We’re trained for exactly that,” he said, “and Aaron, I want to thank you for giving my dad this job.” He shook my hand. I felt like I was an uncle. When the marine left, Jacob came over to me. “I hope you don’t mind that we’re here,” he said, “I thought that late Sunday would be a good time. We didn’t intend to crash your party—and I couldn’t stop him from wearing the tallit, it was the only way I could get him to come see you.”

“Whatever it takes,” I said. “Is he acting any better?”

“Worse,” the son said. “He’s canceled the electricity effective September 15, he’s giving us a week for shiva. He has nothing anymore; he’s turned himself into a waiting room.” Across the parking lot from us, Mr. Fisher stood. He didn’t take his eyes off me. “The doctor told me to bring him here,” Jacob said, “he advised me to do anything that would make Dad active. Staying home and counting the days is the worst.”

Elario was so drunk that I didn’t know if he could tell Carlos from Morris Fisher when he brought the marine over to shake hands with the old man.

“Look at him,” Elario said, “he’s in uniform, and you’re not.” Elario had started drinking early, as soon as the beer arrived. The guy was flying and he had a woman hanging from his armpit. This was the first time I had seen Elario with his old crowd and I wasn't crazy about the way he was acting, but it was his party, his marine. I spent a little time with my mother and Luisa, and then I heard el diablo's pipes even before the crowd parted to make space for Elario on the lot. "The marine has got to make his plane," Elario said. Carlos waved to everyone as he lowered himself into the front bucket seat.

"Grandpa," Elario yelled to Mr. Fisher, "have you ever been in a car that has a chandelier?"

"No," Morris Fisher said.

"Well, come on—*vamonos*—you're in for some thrills." The old man hesitated, but he did seem interested.

"I'm only going with Aaron Evans—are you going?" he asked me.

"No," I said. Even though I sold Elario and the rest of the crowd their kits and blocks, riding in their lowered cars made me feel like I was skateboarding on my back. Elario came over to help Mr. Fisher into the car. "You don't need Aaron," he said, "I'm your man."

"Tell Dad to go," Jacob Fisher urged me, "it will be good for him."

Mr. Fisher waited for my approval and I knew that all I had to do was nod my head and he'd let Elario load him into the back seat. But even though he called me the angel of death, I sure didn't want him to get into Elario's car.

"You've still got some time," I said, "why not wait for me?"

"Okay," he said, "I'll wait." He turned away from Elario and walked to the only table on the lot. He sat down there next to my mother and Luisa, who were still eating. Jacob Fisher ran at me, his fists clenched. "What's with you," he said, "you're playing right into his fantasy. I don't get it."

The Chevy backed slowly onto Fannin Street and then took off. At the freeway ramp, three inches above ground and with eight speakers blasting, Elario merged her onto I-10 aiming toward Baghdad. I walked over to the table, took my mother's hand and pulled her along. When Mr. Fisher asked if I wanted him, too, I told him that he was more than welcome to come along for the ride.

Strawberry Shortcake

WIFE OR NO WIFE, bankrupt or not, on Sunday Sidney Goodman, the carwash king of Las Vegas, pointed his Chrysler LeBaron convertible toward Heritage Estates. There, surrounded by flowers in bloom and mostly healthy fellow seniors, his mother awaited her boy.

It hadn't been easy to get her into this posh apartment complex. Heritage Estates, with its hotel-like lobby, its pool and exercise room, was, as Janet, the manager, liked to say, "An upscale apartment building whose elevator doors close a tad slower. We're here for active seniors." It would not be great for Janet's marketing campaign to feature his mother, Lucy Goodman, most active in the elegant lobby as she attacked her caregiver with a fork. This she had done once, but that was in a previous building and with another caregiver. It had been a while and he thought those outbursts of senile rage were over, but who could know?

By the time her only child brought her to Las Vegas from Orange County Lucy Goodman no longer knew the difference between one place and another. States or even countries could matter less; even hot and cold was too subtle a matter for her. She might raise her hand when they walked outdoors to block the sun from her eyes. Sweat might run along the lines of her furrowed brow. "Are you too warm, Mama? Should we go inside?"

"I'm not hot, I need my coat."

Sidney was used to it. He expected little from her, had done his mourning in the early months, right after her diagnosis, when all the aberrations were so painful and surprising. Dr. Portnoy suggested testing at the geriatric institute, and Sidney accompanied her. The psychologist asked her name and date of birth. "Why is she bothering me with this, Sidney? Didn't you tell her all of this already?"

"Mrs. Goodman, could you tell me your telephone number please?"

"Sidney, tell her my number."

"No, Mrs. Goodman, I need to hear from you, not from Sidney."

"Sidney, she doesn't believe that I know my telephone number. Who do you think I am, Miss? Do you know that I worked for twenty-two years at Macy's in many departments. I sold luggage and gifts and what we used to call notions when I was a young woman."

"Mrs. Goodman, just your phone number."

"If I want you to know my phone number, I'll tell you my phone number. Sidney, why should she have my number? I don't want her to call. I get enough of those annoying calls—every day I get them from—you know—from—from—people."

Sidney listened; he had known for sometime that she was off. He teased her when the frozen strawberries she served turned out to be tomatoes, he laughed with her when she didn't remember how long she had been married, didn't laugh at all when she couldn't remember her late husband's name, and began seriously to worry when a neighbor called him: "Your mom is driving on the wrong side of the road, like she's in England."

In the early stages, Sidney flew down to Orange County more often, took the car first, then the credit cards and the checkbook. It went slowly. Two years before he'd had to hire a day companion and then two more years of troubleshooting from distance. When it became an everyday problem he decided to bring her to Vegas.

"Your phone number please," the psychologist insisted. While his mother stalled, the woman took notes. She had infinite patience, had been waiting five minutes for that telephone number. Sidney timed it on his watch. "I'll give you a hint," the psychologist finally said, "your number starts with an area code, which is a three-digit number. I'm going to give you the first number." She paused for dramatic effect. "The number is—2."

Lucy looked at her son, desperate, a child at a spelling bee. Here was the chance she had been waiting for, the big clue and it didn't help a bit. "Sidney, tell her." He had to bite his lip, kept his teeth pushing down so hard that it hurt. "Let's move on, then," the psychologist said. And so they did, moved on, Sidney and his mom, moving on, they still were.

"How long can she live this way?" Sidney asked the doctor.

"That's hard to say," Dr. Portnoy told him, "a few years I'd guess, it depends on her general health and the kind of care she gets."

Six years later, at the beginning of the new millennium, she was still moving on, munching as she went on tuna fish and baked apples and waiting, always for her boy to take her for a ride.

For the mandatory new residents' interview at Heritage Estates Sidney admitted in advance only that Mom (in public he called her that, in private, Mama) had a few memory problems. Janet led them into a conference room, served coffee from a silver-plated samovar. A painting of a young woman frolicking with a horse decorated one wall, a color photo of a healthy fellow in leather shorts climbing a mountain was on another wall. Sidney got it. They weren't crazy about sickies in this senior residence, they preferred the frolickers, the mountain climbers. They also wanted three thousand dollars a month, and from the looks of the lobby and the mailboxes without names on them Sidney thought his mother had a chance. He placed his check, two months rent plus damage deposit, on the conference table. This was Vegas, he led with a strong opener. Then a little bluff, "Mom is lots of fun," he said, "but she's not going to live alone, that's why we want a two-bedroom."'

Lucy looked at her coffee. She had pixielike features—Tinkerbell they used to call her at Macy's because she was so fast and cute and jovial and such a busybody, dropping her dust all over other people's lives. "Is there sugar?" she asked.

"Of course," Janet said, "I'll get you some." A good question, score one for Mama, Sidney thought. "Drink your coffee and keep quiet," he whispered as Janet roamed the back rooms for sugar. She returned with a crystal-bowlful of packets.

"As I was saying, my mother will have a live-in companion, a woman of Spanish descent." He wanted Janet to imagine an Andalusian lady, thin-lipped, long-legged, the kind of person who could talk to the mountain climber in the photograph, maybe even join him on his next expedition. "I want my mother to have company and I'm so busy— do you know Panama Pete's carwash? Yes, that's me and no, that's not my face on the sign." He reached into his pocket for the free carwash coupons, placed a thick stack on the coffee table right next to his check.

"What are you doing here?" Lucy asked her interviewer.

"I'm the building manager," Janet said, "I'm here to handle complaints and to make sure that there aren't too many of them." She laughed.

"Why did you pish in this coffee?" Lucy Goodman asked.

"Stop teasing, Mom," Sidney said. He smiled at Janet. "Mother is used to instant coffee. If you don't like it, Mom, just leave it. Okay."

"I want clean water," she said.

"Not a problem," Janet said. Sidney wanted this over as quickly as possible.

"Her helper, of course, will take care of serving and everything else, Mom will just hang around and have fun, won't you, Mom?"

Her helper, the Spanish lady, Rosita, came to the carwash one day with her son Ysidro, Sidney's best ragboy. "My mother needs to work," Ysidro said, "she's strong, just came from Guatemala, six months." Rosita, almost as broad as she was tall, extended a hand. "I like to wash the cars, very clean," she said. He wasn't crazy about a middle-aged woman at the carwash, but once she was decked out in an oversize Pete's T-shirt and a baseball cap, you had to look close to see that she was a female. And Ysidro was great, had been at Pete's for three years, the best ever of ragboys, never missed a day. If Ysidro wanted his mother to work, what better recommendation could she have.

And Rosita turned out to be a bull. She did the low work, vacuuming around the brake pedal and the accelerator, the quick initial cleanups. She'd been at Pete's for a few months when Sidney brought his mother to Las Vegas. When he offered, Rosita jumped at the new job.

He had to find a new building because Sheridan Square, far less deluxe than Heritage Estates, but more than good enough, was in the process of evicting Mama and Rosita. Sidney agreed to pay an extra month's rent to keep the reason quiet. The first time that Lucy called 911 was no big deal; it was two in the afternoon and the responding officers laughed it off. They made a quick check of the apartment and that was it, no commotion at all. The second time, about a month later, she called at 3 AM, told the dispatcher that a man was hiding in her bathtub. Rosita, snoring in her own room, didn't answer the doorbell. The police had to wait for the manager. When they entered Lucy screamed, so did Rosita. The activity woke other residents, and the whole floor searched for the intruder. When Lucy spoke to the police she had no memory of the call, the man, or the bathub. Sidney took her to the doctor, and they changed one of the tranquilizers that the doctor said could have been causing hallucinations.

Janet looked at his mother, awaiting any questions. Sidney drummed his fingers, let them move closer to his check and the carwash coupons. "Could I show you apartment 212," Janet said. She led them to the elevator. Sidney praised his mother's speed. "Look, she beat us to the elevator, and she could take the stairs, too."

"Let's go," Lucy Goodman said, ready to demonstrate. Sidney held her back. On the second floor, at apartment 211, a woman stood in the doorway; coal black eyes, a stylish dress, tall and distinguished looking, Sidney didn't like to see this. Way too much for Mama, he thought. "This is Birdie Simmons, she's been here for over a year. Birdie, I'd like to introduce Mrs. Goodman and her son, Sidney. Mrs. Goodman might be your new neighbor in 212."

Birdie smiled and followed them into 212 even though Sidney didn't want her there, feared that she might rile Lucy up, since his mother had no idea that she was moving. But Birdie said nothing and neither did his mother. Green carpeting, a small efficient kitchen, a dinette, two bathrooms. "We'll take it," Sidney said, "I'll sign the lease."

"Do you live here?" his mother asked Birdie.

"I live next door," Birdie said. She spoke very softly.

"Where's the furniture?" Lucy asked. "Did you steal the furniture?"

"Your furniture is going to look great here," Sidney said. He led her out the door before she could say anything else. "Your couch, your bedroom set—and will Rosita ever be happy with that second bathroom."

Two years later, Birdie had become a better companion than Rosita, almost a Siamese twin. Except for sleep, Birdie spent all day with his mother.

Still, as much as he liked her, Sidney didn't want Birdie along on Sundays; he didn't want Rosita either, but it was a package deal. No more just Mom and Sidney; those days were over. Sometimes when he thought about it, it seemed to him that his mother had lost even more privacy than memory, but he did what he could.

The four of them, top down, cruised through the suburbs, which Sidney knew less well than the industrial area, where at certain corners the day laborers gathered. Sidney went there to pick up a few extra ragboys whenever he needed them.

Today he had no heart for cruising. He changed his mind about the Strip and drove directly into Denny's lot, held open the back door while the ladies grabbed at knobs and buttons in their struggle to exit.

"Your ladyships," he said, "the king and queen of Denny's await you at booth 8. There will be an exquisite state dinner featuring game birds captured on the royal estate and prepared within minutes after their painless execution." He tried to entertain them, but his mouth began to feel dry. Rosita walked alongside Birdie; Sidney escorted his mother. They didn't stop to wait for the hostess; menus in hand, she motioned them directly to booth 8, the oversize one at the rear of the restaurant.

"Panama Pete and his girls," she said. "It must be Sunday. How's everyone today?"

Birdie nodded, lowered her eyes; Rosita grabbed the menus. She had been hungry since she finished what his mother left at breakfast.

"We'll have poached pheasant," Sidney said, "with Chateauneuf du Pape."

"Four tuna melts and four Cokes?" the hostess asked.

Sidney nodded. He used his British accent at Denny's; at Fresh Choice he liked to play the Russian. Three years of drama school and the only character acting he did these days was in the restaurant with his girls.

His mother grabbed one of the menus out of her son's hands. "I want that," she said pointing to strawberry shortcake with whipped cream on the right side of the plastic menu.

"You want something else, too?" Sidney asked. "Just name it, anything you want."

Lucy's eyes flashed. "No, I want that," she said. She tried to stand, but the angle of the bench kept her from getting erect. Sidney reached out to steady her.

"Take it easy," he said. "If you want strawberry shortcake, you'll get strawberry shortcake. I thought you should have some protein, too, but if that's what you want—hey."

Slowly he had learned to give up being reasonable with her. The last vestige was food—maybe because she had been such an exacting mother as far as diet. Raw carrots in water always in the refrigerator for snacks, homemade bread, whole wheat crackers, nothing but the healthiest for her Sidney, and he was still trying to give her the same. He knew that it made no sense. Why a balanced diet for an unbalanced woman? And what harm would it do her to eat the sugary dessert? For that matter, what harm if she ate the plate, the spoon, the napkin—all of red-vinyl booth number 8. She was immune. Nothing would harm her; nothing could harm her, and if she wasn't a good girl, if she didn't have her balanced lunch, she would have that much less energy to listen to KRBC or the Spanish-language soap operas.

"Three tuna melts and one strawberry shortcake," he told the waitress.

"Sorry," she said, "no shortcake."

"How's that possible?" Sidney asked. "It takes up half the menu."

"No strawberries," she said. "You want the cake and the whipped cream, you can have that."

Sidney looked at his mother, not sure whether she understood the new information. While the waitress waited he translated, pointed to the picture on the menu. "They have this, but not this," he said. As he pointed, he tried to use the palm of his hand to obscure the enormous red strawberries.

"I want strawberry shortcake," she said.

"I know you do, but they don't have strawberries. So do you want just shortcake? Look at this beautiful cake and all the whipped cream you want. I'll bet the waitress will even give you extra whipped cream." He looked at the waitress, who was anxious to get away.

"Sure," she said, "all the whipped cream you can eat." She tapped her foot and held the pencil against her order pad.

Lucy tried to stand, but again could only make it three-quarters of the way. "I want the strawberries," she said.

The waitress looked at Sidney.

"Do you have any other kind of berries?" he asked.

The waitress shook her head. "We never have other kinds, just strawberries."

"That's right," Lucy said, "strawberries."

Sidney began to think of moving them out of the booth, back to the car, and over to the IHOP on the other side of the freeway.

"Let's go get strawberries somewhere else," he announced. "Sorry," he said to the waitress. He took a five-dollar bill out of his wallet.

The waitress shook her head. "Not necessary," she said. "You can tip me next time—when we've got what you want." She smiled and walked away.

Sidney held out his hand to his mother.

"You're not taking me out," she yelled. She pointed to the menu; then she held it with both hands and pressed the photograph of the berries against her chest.

Rosita tried to pry it loose. "We going to other restaurant," she said.

Lucy pushed her away, gripped her menu even tighter.

It had become a life-and-death matter. Every so often something became this crucial. There was no way to predict what would set her off. When she couldn't find a calendar or a bedspread she might scream and cry and turn pale and go into a semicollapse on the couch. At her apartment Sidney or Rosita would put a cold washcloth against her forehead, and sometimes they could even come up with the item that drove her to despair. In the restaurant Sidney just wanted to avoid trouble. Denny's wasn't crowded, but it would still be embarrassing.

He looked at Rosita. "Ready?"

She nodded, stood; so did Birdie. The two of them walked toward the exit. The waitress, busy at another table, waved. When Birdie and Rosita were at the car, Sidney pointed to them, waved through the window. Then he turned to his mother.

"They're ready," he said. "I'll race you to the car." He had a big smile on, the kind he used when a customer lost some trim to the high-pressure spray and Sidney came out to reassure that Panama Pete's would take care of the damage. That was easy: some Superglue, a rubber hammer, at worst a few minutes in the body shop—there was one around the corner.

"Mama," he said, "we're going to get you the best strawberry shortcake in Las Vegas. Take that menu along. We'll show them at IHOP so they'll know exactly what you want."

He kept talking, but he could see that it was too late. She had pulled back like a dog with teeth bared, ready to jump. The energy was loose; it had to go somewhere. There were only four glasses of ice water on the table so she couldn't do that much damage. Sidney stood waiting at the front of the booth, but she had crouched, pulled her knees up using them too as protection for her precious menu. Sidney kept his cheerful look and calm voice, but he was considering a quick strike, a reach across the booth to pick her up like a child having a tantrum. With her knees up she was almost a ball; he could probably do it. Quick and violent, he would get her out of Denny's and try to control the damage once he reached the car. By the time they got to IHOP she wouldn't remember anything; he knew that. She wouldn't even want the strawberry shortcake. But for now the cake had become the meaning and purpose of life. By now Sidney knew that. As crazy as it was—the cake, the calendar, the bedspread—whatever it was mattered to her more than the world. She would have cut the throat of her beloved Sidney to get these berries, would have unleashed a nuclear bomb, poisoned wells, beheaded children. This was it: pure will and it was no act. The time she thought he had stolen her bedspread she went at him with a knife. He had no problem taking it from her, and a half-hour later when he had calmed her down he told her, "It's a sickness. I want you to understand that it's a sickness." She looked as glum as she should after such an outburst. He was getting through to her. He put an arm around her. "A sickness," he said, "that's what it is."

"Yes," she said, "go to a doctor. Maybe he can cure you. Go to the best doctor. I'll pay for it." Her eyes were full of love.

He surveyed the booth again. He would have to reach across and lift her straight up. Once he had her he knew she would put up a fight, biting, scratching—she weighed 102 pounds, but in fury she could do damage to him, maybe his eyes, and he could easily break a rib or two or worse if he squeezed her too tightly.

She knew what he planned. She had lost memory but not cunning. When it came to physical geography, to plotting, to getting her body in the best position to resist, she became a clever tactician. She dropped her legs, uncurled herself; then she pulled all four water glasses in front of her as a line of defense. She found the napkin holder as well. Everything Denny's had to offer, she used. He decided that force wouldn't work. He sat down opposite her, said nothing. She had already won—there were no stakes, but she had won. They would stay here until it passed. The urge for strawberries or whatever strawberries had come to signify would not be permanent, and after all, what was the hurry? Sunday was the day he gave her; a booth at Denny's was no worse than listening to the radio in her apartment. Without Birdie and Rosita he had her to himself in the booth. He touched nothing. She had claimed the menu, the napkins, the water glasses—let her have them.

"You're the queen of the booth," he finally said. "All of this belongs to you, but could I have just one napkin?"

She nodded. He had an opening now, a way to begin the process of distracting her. He used the napkin to wipe up a few drops of water on the tabletop. She watched, still hypervigilant. He pushed the napkin back and forth until the thin paper balled up. Then he laid it, an offering, beside the water glasses.

She looked but didn't touch, not for a few seconds. Then it became irresistible. She touched the wadded napkin, pulled it to her, another treasure, another reason to value this world.

"Mama," Sidney said. He whispered. Right there in Denny's—sitting across from a high-school athlete whose big legs were blocking the aisle while he stared at his girlfriend, who seemed as absorbed in the menu as his mother had been—right there in public view if anyone wanted to look, he leaned across and with one finger touched the plastic-coated photograph of strawberries.

"They're not so fresh," he said. "I don't think they'll last. What do you think?"

Slowly, very slowly, he turned the page as she loosened her grip enough to let the menu open. "Smell them," he said, moving the laminated paper close to her nose. "These aren't the kind of berries you buy. You buy the nice fresh ones from Mrs. Jenosi at the farmers market. I think we should wait and go there like we always do."

She considered the possibility.

"Mrs. Jenosi would never sell you berries like this," he said. "They put the fresh ones on top and underneath"—he pointed to the mounds of whipped cream—"underneath there's nothing but mold. You'd be throwing away your money. Do you want to throw away your money?"

"No," she said. She put down the menu.

She let him hold her hand as she slid out of the booth. The long-legged teenager tucked in his legs. Sidney and his mother walked past the arcade games, past the gripper arm that almost picked up stuffed animals, past the cashier and the Leukemia Society change cup, past the last danger spot, an enlarged strawberry-filled menu near the swinging door. He blocked that menu with his back as he opened the door.

"Mama," he said, "we made it." He put his arms around her, raised her tiny body a few inches off the ground. "Congratulations! We made it out of there. Are you happy?"

Her face lit up. "I'm happy," she said. "I'm always happy."

Adventures in Dementia

JENNY GOODMAN, a perky eighty-four, with clear blue eyes, high cheekbones, and a nice set of natural teeth, remembered her only child, Sidney, but not her husband. The one-time tire store owner and man about the house had been dead since 1980; still, Sidney wondered, why no dad when Elvis, and President Kennedy, and even Elaine Claiborne, her former neighbor, sometimes roamed the drafty aisles of Mom's brain.

His mother's total loss of husband memories made him feel as if he was losing his father again, this time without a minyan of his father's friends, without even a corpse, and a quarter of a century past grief. On his regular Sunday visits to his mother he sometimes played "name that husband" to pass the tedious hours, but when he got more serious about stirring her memory he changed the name to "project Dad," hoping that the word project would light up some neglected neurons.

How happy his mother had once been to help with those grade school assignments, the big ones, those dignified enough to be called projects. After dinner she had scrubbed the dining-room table so that he could spread out his clean poster board. She had provided the glue and the beans or peas or pieces of dried fruit that he required. She had cut out the magazine pictures to illustrate his work as together they had labeled the major exports of Venezuela and described the life cycle of the influenza virus. Now, forty-some years later, they would do it again. "Project Dad," Sidney called out like a master of ceremonies, "let's go for it."

But, even for his son, Harold Goodman was no easy retrieval. He had come to seem not so much a father as a business partner who had made a miscalculation by cashing out too early. Sidney hung onto sales records for three years, tax returns seven years—Dad had been gone far beyond any statute of limitations. Yearly, Sidney granted his father the lifetime achievement award, the *Yizkor* memorial prayer as one rabbi after another droned out the same words, "Our loved ones live on in our memory."

"Maybe not," Sidney thought. His doubts made him glad that he didn't understand the familiar Hebrew words that he repeated as if they really could connect him to some remnant of his father.

Sidney and Jenny started the project with the obvious choice, photographs. He went through her old scrapbooks, pulling the prints loose from the little black edges that she had glued to the page. "Look at this one," Sidney said as he pointed to a muscular Harold Goodman at Coney Island in black trunks and a white T-shirt, *Lifeguard* written across his chest. Jenny in a swimsuit with skirt stood shyly next to him.

"And there he is, your husband with Richie Ashburn of the Phillies, when Richie came to the store to buy a set of radials." Sidney pointed to the Kodak print. His mother smiled like a Buddhist monk. "Which one is dad?" Sidney asked.

Jenny pointed to the Phillies centerfielder, in 1950 known as one of the whiz kids. She was correct about half the time, as likely to pick her husband as to find George Washington when Sidney flipped a quarter, something he did on some visits because it seemed to hold her interest and involved less effort than talking.

When the photographs turned out to be only images connected to paper and color but not to people, they migrated to dress-up. Sidney impersonated his father with what remained of Harold Goodman's wardrobe, one dark green sport coat saved because twenty-four years ago it had fit him. Now, modeling it for Jenny, the son had to drape it over his shoulders as if it was a bullfighter's cape. But Harold's Panama still looked fine, and when Sidney tilted the angle of the hat and placed a Lucky Strike between his lips and even lit it with the noisy click of his father's original Zippo, he almost felt like it really was about 1978 and being alive was still a normal everyday event for Harold Goodman.

"Hey, Jen," he said to his mother, "here I am. It's been awhile, hasn't it?"

He felt like an idiot and couldn't have done this if anyone else had been watching, but Jenny Goodman did not judge him. "Name that husband," Sidney said. His mother furrowed her brow. She looked thoughtful, but that was as far as she went.

"Am I Harold Goodman?" he asked.

After a long pause Jenny said, "I'm hungry," and looked toward the kitchen.

Aside from his five-hour stint on Sundays while the caregiver, Luisa, visited her own family, Sidney hardly thought about his mother. He didn't discuss her at work, and even his ex-wife, Ruth, with whom he was on friendly terms, had stopped asking him about Jenny. Safe and well cared for, his mother existed as a statistic; on paper a resident and taxpayer of Las Vegas. As recently as the 2000 election she had gone to the polls, perhaps to vote.

In the lobby of her apartment building people sometimes nodded to Jenny Goodman, and an occasional Safeway clerk wished her a nice day. Darlene, the hairdresser, told her that she was still beautiful, and Luisa's children, when they visited their own mother, sometimes brought trinkets, like barrettes, for her roommate.

After Sidney had failed with photography and wardrobe, one Sunday afternoon he tried theater. While his mother at the kitchen table sipped decaf, Sidney narrated a story his father had loved to tell. "It's 1950 and we're living in Detroit, both of us, you with your Aunt Rose, me above the shoe store on Livernois Avenue. We're at Briggs Stadium. You've been here once before when we sat in the bleachers. Today we're in a box seat just off the third-base line on the lower deck three rows behind the Ford Motor Company box, what do you think of that? Harold Goodman and Jenny Stern as close to the field as the Fords, only those anti-Semites didn't work overtime to pay for their tickets. George Kell is at bat, and on the mound, Bob Feller, the fireballing right-hander of the Cleveland Indians." Sidney tried to sound like his father or like an actor, or at least like a radio announcer. He went to one knee, took from his pocket the dark blue velvet box, held it in the air to show the crowd, then he opened it slowly right before Jenny's eyes as he waited for that big moment in her life to work again, as if on instant replay. The story was one of the staples of his childhood. His father narrated, his mother blushed, and little Sidney had basked in the details. Jenny Stern said yes and then, as if to seal that joyous moment, the Tigers went on to win the game in eleven innings. Harold Goodman always ended the story with a hug; he loved the story, loved his wife. Sidney, for total reenactment, squeezed her tiny shoulders.

His mother looked at the four-carat cubic zirconium jewel that Sidney had bought at Target. "It's a ring," she said.

"Who gave it to you?" Sidney asked. "Tell me that."

"You did," she said.

"Okay," Sidney said, "and who am I?" He would settle for it if she conflated father and son, that would do it, that would be fine. He just wanted the words *Harold Goodman* to cross her lips again.

"You're you," Jenny said, and though her son bombarded her with choices for the ring bearer, ranging from Harold Goodman to Winston Churchill and William Shakespeare, Jenny merely wrinkled her nose at all the candidates, her husband as impossible to name as the nameless one, the creator of heaven and earth.

Sidney tried not to blame her—of course it wasn't her fault, dementia was dementia and even without it normal everyday life piled up more memories than a person could hold onto. In the quarter century since his father had died, leaving to his son a tire store and thirty-thousand-dollar inventory, Sidney had added much inventory of his own, three more stores; an ex-wife, a few serious lady friends whom Sidney himself had mostly forgotten.

And it wasn't just his father, some of his own friends were beginning to leave this world, most recently his tennis partner, David Evans, who thought it was indigestion in the second set and went home to begin his eternal nap. Sidney mourned him like a brother, twelve years of once-a-week tennis except for vacations. Sidney comforted the widow, Sharon. At first only comfort. Then, what could he do? She cried in his arms. After a month, after two months, he had to recognize that his arms were not separate from the rest of him. He felt guilty; she said that she felt worse. Who could know why things just happened without any intentions? He thought of the line from the Firestone commercial, "where the rubber meets the road." He liked that line so much that he sometimes regretted not carrying Firestone.

As his life rolled along he was aware of growing older, yet at fifty-one he still daydreamed about women and about what seemed to be his future, as if he were a boy deciding what job he would take or what college he would attend. Still, he had learned a lot in almost thirty years in the tire business—he knew how important it was to set reasonable goals. For his stores he aimed at 12–15 percent and if he got a little more, fine. So he knew better than to aim for complete retrieval of Dad. He wasn't asking for intact memories, no personality, no emotion—just the name. How much more modest could a target be? But, so far, the thing was unsolvable, like his divorce, like the Firestone SUV tire recall, just out of his hands.

Still, the problem bothered him every Sunday as he felt himself becoming angry at his helpless mother for this ridiculous version of marital failure. The rest of the week he was fine: tire sales were good, he felt well enough, and Sharon had finally stopped lighting a memorial candle after every time they made love.

What troubled him most about the father problem, Sidney decided, was the lack of a plan, what to do next. One Sunday while his mother stared into her coffee cup, Sidney on a paper towel listed some possible choices:

> A trip—to the tire store? to Detroit? a Seance? electric shock?

Then came his moment of inspiration. As he considered various scientific interventions, he thought of Dr. Nepenthe, and against what Sidney thought would be long odds, he managed to locate and contact the man. The doctor, surprisingly, took Sunday appointments, so Sidney didn't have to rearrange his mother's schedule.

The following Sunday, when he walked into the apartment to pick up his mother, Luisa and Jenny were watching El Gordo on the Mexican channel. "Looka heem," Luisa said. The fat comedian was trying to limbo beneath a broomstick held by two almost naked young women. He leered as he limboed.

"That's you," Jenny Goodman said to her son.

Sidney didn't argue. "Yes it is," he said, "and it looks like I'm having fun." El Gordo snaked his chins beneath the bar, and as he did, the girls dropped the broomstick to applaud and jiggle their flesh. Sidney went to the closet for a light jacket in case his mother complained about the air-conditioning in his Chrysler. Mom walked crisply to the car, a fifteen-minute ride on the freeway as refreshing to her as crossing the Atlantic.

Sidney located the doctor's name on the directory of a shabby stucco building. When the doctor answered the door, Sidney recognized the face immediately. "They used to advertise you on TV all the time," Sidney said. "Which casino was it?"

"The Sands," Dr. Nepenthe said. "I worked at the Sands for thirteen years. Now they feature nothing but large breasts and animals." He offered his hand to Sidney.

"Is Nepenthe really your name?" Sidney asked

"I changed it legally in 1962," he said. "That's what everyone called me, so why not?"

Dr. Nepenthe seemed to be in his seventies, or maybe even as old as Jenny. A few straggly hairs lay scattered across the top of his scalloped head. He wore a gray suit that needed pressing. His wingtip shoes were untied. He noticed Sidney staring at his feet.

"When you get to my age loafers are the best. I've got a pair." Sidney held his mother by the elbow waiting for directions, but Dr. Nepenthe ignored his client to search beneath the couch for his loafers. "Try to find anything when you really need it," he said. Sidney coughed. "When I called I wasn't sure if you were retired or still a practicing hypnotist."

"Both," the doctor said. "I'm out of show business, but I still work every day." He handed Sidney a business card, artfully shaped. "Dogs?" Sidney asked.

"Yes sir, dogs," Dr. Nepenthe said, "what they say is true, they really are man's best friend."

Sidney led his mother to the couch, the only open seating in the living room. There were two hardback chairs in the adjacent dinette, but both held piles of newspaper. Sidney had mailed, in advance, a check for two hundred dollars, as Dr. Nepenthe had requested. Two hundred for someone who once had his own act at the Sands had seemed like a bargain, but, looking around, Sidney wasn't so sure.

"So I take it from the card that you hypnotize both dogs and people?"

"Of course," the doctor said, "but the people moment has passed." Sidney decided not to dwell on this. "I told you what I'd like her to recall," he said. Dr. Nepenthe walked to a small notepad near his wall phone. "Yes, I've got the name right here," he said, "let's give it the old college try and we'll see what happens."

"Can I watch?" Sidney asked.

"That is the question I have been asked more than any other throughout my career. It's strange, isn't it, people have been watching me for years and there's nothing to see. It's all invisible, all right here." He pointed to his head. "Watch all you want but no talking." He motioned for Sidney to stand near the door. "Did you bring a recording of your father's voice?"

"No," Sidney said, "was I supposed to?"

Dr. Nepenthe shrugged. "It didn't occur to me," Sidney said. "I don't even think such a thing exists.

"Well, what did he sound like? Can you do an imitation?"

Sidney, in his mind, could hear his father but not as a voice. When Sidney sold the house and moved his mother to the Green Meadows apartment complex and hired Luisa, he gave dozens of boxes to Goodwill. He recalled old reel-to-reel tapes; maybe in one of them there had been a recording of his father's voice. Maybe someone bought it for fifty cents without any knowledge of what a treasure some would consider it to hear Harold Goodman.

"I remember what he sounded like but I can't describe it, maybe he sounded like I do."

"Could be," the doctor said, "but if it's not exact I wouldn't go there."

From the shelf of his bookcase, Nepenthe retrieved what looked like a shoebox with a cord dangling from one end. A few round disks balanced atop the machine.

"What did the man smell like?" the doctor asked.

Instantly Sidney had it—Boraxo, the powdered hand soap. Sidney could not only smell it, he could see the soapy foam dribbling toward his father's elbows as he raised damp arms to a towel.

"He smelled like Boraxo." Sidney tried to say it nonchalantly but his voice quivered with feeling.

"Not a choice," the doctor said. He examined his disks. "Let's see, I've got lemongrass, peppermint, lavender, and patchouli."

"Those are herbal teas," Sidney said, "nobody smells like that."

"It's what I've got," the doctor said. "They don't make Boraxo for the Aromamaster. I don't think they even make it at all. Which one do you want?"

"Lemongrass," Sidney said without enthusiasm. Dr. Nepenthe slipped one of the 3-inch disks into the machine and within seconds Sidney could almost taste the lemongrass.

"It's too strong at first, but it will even out after a few minutes," Dr. Nepenthe said. "I use it to set the mood. Next, there's this." He opened the cover of a portable hi-fi and placed the needle on a record.

"I know what you're thinking," the doctor said. "The old coot is stuck in 1970. Surprise, I've got CDs wall to wall but that's not what your mom and dad listened to, is it? So I borrowed this for the afternoon. You've heard of Johnny Mathis?"

The doctor turned to Jenny Goodman, comfortable on the couch, her fingers occasionally pulling at fibers.

"Would you like to hear the deep voiced Mr. Vaughn Monroe, late of the Tommy Dorsey band?" The doctor asked her, "Or would it be the more romantic and sweet-toned Johnny Mathis?"

Jenny Goodman smiled at her hypnotist without expressing a preference.

"Okay," Dr. Nepenthe said, "then I'll choose. Here we go."

The amplified voice of Johnny Mathis filled the one-bedroom townhouse. As the singer crooned "Chances Are," Dr. Nepenthe moved one of the newspaper piles to the floor and brought the chair closer so that he could sit directly in front of his patient, who expressed no interest in the music or the hypnotist.

The doctor closed his eyes and let his upper body sway to the rhythm. After a few minutes Sidney could hear his mother's deep breathing as loud as the Aromamaster.

When the Johnny Mathis song ended, the doctor patted Jenny's shoulder to make sure that she was asleep, then he went to his bedroom, returning with yet another device, a portable tape player. The hypnotist pressed "Play" and Sidney heard the doctor's raspy taped voice call out "sit," followed by a long pause and a repetition, "I said, sit." There were a few more "sits," then the doctor's recorded voice ordered, "heel." The hypnotist listened to his own voice as he watched his patient sleep.

"Do you have the right tape?" Sidney whispered loudly. The doctor raised a finger to his lips but Sidney ignored the signal. "Let's try a person tape, Harold Goodman was a person, maybe I didn't make that clear."

"Species doesn't matter," the doctor said, "neither do words."

Sidney found himself growing angry. "If words don't matter why are we listening to your commands?"

The doctor turned his back to Sidney. "You see why I like to work with dogs." He stopped the tape recorder. "Are you going to let me continue or not? It's your dime."

"All I'm trying to say is she's my mother, not my pet. She's lost a lot but she's still a person, that's all I'm trying to say. Treat her like a person."

The hypnotist turned to face his imagined audience. "The gentleman thinks that species is the problem. Is that what you think?" He put a hand to his ear signaling the crowd to let him hear by applause what they thought the problem might be.

"We were not a pet family," Sidney said, "not even a goldfish—hypnotized, not hypnotized, I don't think about pets at all." Sidney tiptoed to the couch, where his mother slept soundly, her head against her shoulder. She would have been better off at home on her own couch. He felt the foolishness of what he was doing. "If we stop now," Sidney asked, "can I get a full refund?"

The doctor rolled his eyes. "I never had a dog who asked for a full refund."

"I'm sorry," Sidney said, "it's not about the money, it just feels as if I should have kept this personal, just between us." The doctor unplugged the Aromamaster. Sidney hesitated. ". . . Okay . . . as long as we're here, go ahead . . . I wish . . ." He found himself unable to finish the sentence. The hypnotist pressed "Play." Sidney could hardly bear to listen as the recording continued with "stay," then proceeded to many repetitions of "lie down."

Sidney tried to ignore the taped commands. Instead of his father he found himself thinking of David Evans. There was Dave, happy with his backhand, listening to the ball as it hit the sweet spot of his racquet. He could hear Dave's voice, but what had they talked about for all those years in the locker room, on the court, as they walked to their cars, when they went out to lunch? Thousands of hours, but what did he remember about his old buddy, who had been gone for less than a year? Once a week with Dave; these days, two or three times a week with Sharon. The memorial prayers, the lit candles, the donations to so many of the disease societies . . .

When the tape finished, Dr. Nepenthe clapped his hands but Jenny slept until the doctor yelled so loudly that he startled Sidney. "Say 'Harold.'"

Jenny Goodman opened her eyes. She looked down at her hands as if trying to remember if these things were what she used to scratch herself or to pick up a spoon. She looked relaxed and not all confused, just busy looking at hands.

"Say 'Harold,'" the doctor ordered again. He didn't look at his patient but began to roll the cord of the Aromamaster, then he placed the Johnny Mathis record back in its sleeve. "These old 33s are worth a fortune if they're in good shape," he said. Sidney ignored him, kept his eyes on his mother.

Jenny opened her mouth and Sidney was sure that he could read her lips—two syllables, everything but the vocalization.

"Say 'Harold,'" the hypnotist repeated matter of factly and Jenny's lips moved toward another two syllable word, this time with sound.

The doctor shook his head, "Not 'hair oil,' say 'Harold.' C'mon sweetie, let's hear the real thing." When she said it Sidney couldn't stop the tears. The doctor looked at him without emotion. "Satisfied?" he asked.

Sidney nodded, but satisfied was not what he felt. He waited for his voice to return. "Can you get her to say, 'my husband'?"

Dr. Nepenthe turned from Sidney to address the audience. "Always something else, isn't it? The man pays for one thing, he tells me exactly what he wants and then he wants more."

"I'm sorry," Sidney said, "don't get me wrong, believe me, I'm grateful for the word."

"That's it then," Dr. Nepenthe said, "session over."

"But I feel like we're just getting started," Sidney said. "Now that I've heard her say his name, it's like the door just opened and I want to see what else is on the other side. I'll pay for overtime." He reached for his wallet

"Not possible," the hypnotist said, "I've got a springer spaniel at 4:30."

"Is there a way for me get her to say his name at home—I mean, can it happen regularly from now on?"

The doctor glared at Sidney. "If I could cure Alzheimer's, would I be hypnotizing dogs?"

On the ride home Sidney checked in the rearview mirror to see if there were any aftereffects of the hypnosis; he noticed none. "You okay, mom?" He asked a few times and then, when he could no longer resist, he gave the order, "Say 'Harold.'" He said it in the slow firm style of Dr. Nepenthe on the tape recording.

No answer from the back seat. Sidney tried twice more, with the same result. "What the hell," he said aloud, "don't worry, Mom, you did just fine, A+. It was a great project. I think you said Harold twice—a hundred bucks a pop and well worth it to get such a good grade in vocabulary, right?"

"Good," his mother said, "I feel good."

"Glad you do," Sidney said, "and I'm proud of you, I really am."

By the time Sidney parked his car in the fifteen-minute loading zone and helped his mother to apartment 318, he decided that he too felt pretty good, although it was hard to know why. His mother had said Harold, but she might as well have barked. And, for Sidney, the word Boraxo had been far more resonant than his father's name. The next time he went to *Yizkor* maybe he would tell the rabbi that brand names are what really live on in the memory of loved ones.

Luisa was already at work in the kitchen making scrambled eggs for dinner. Sidney handed the caretaker her weekly paycheck, relieved as always to be leaving his mother's care to someone else. He gave Jenny a final kiss on the top of her thin white hair, made sure that she had the TV remote control close beside her, and was at the door, already thinking about what movie he and Sharon would go to that evening when his mother, in a steady clear voice, called out, "Stay."

Sidney turned to look at her. She had moved her own gaze from the television to her son, a businessman with evening plans.

"Stay," she said once more.

"Mama," Sidney said, "I'll see you next week. You've got everything you need, the television, your meals, Luisa—." He walked back to the couch, put the remote control into her right hand. "Be a good girl, I love you."

"Stay," she said a third time, and though Sidney knew that the word was mechanical, and intended for dogs, he understood that the command encompassed her husband, her son, all those who would flee, and those already gone. He hesitated at the door, and it required the greatest effort of his life to disobey.

Talker

VANESSA HAD A hard time with the truth, she also had hair issues, and if there was ever conflict between hair and truth . . . Well, hair happened, things happened, and when I got angry at her for not showing up as scheduled she took my reaction into account as part of the natural order. "There's never been a time in the world without trouble and there never will be—it's from God, like love."

It wasn't love that kept me from firing her. I needed Vanessa. She fed and bathed Ginny, played with her, and at least in theory, met the school bus drop-off at 3:15. To me it seemed obvious that the needs of a seven-year-old in a wheelchair trumped a hair appointment or having your car CD player repaired or even a trip to the bank, but my perspective, Vanessa said, was limited by my circumstance, an uptight white man.

"The world don't fall apart if I'm five minutes late," she said, "the bus driver can wait, Ginny can wait, and you don't have to start screaming at me like I'm some kind of criminal. You want me to leave—I'll leave right now."

I had already fired her once, and on that occasion she stood in the kitchen, car keys in hand, coat on, but waiting a few seconds so the consequences of my actions could sink in. She had positioned Ginny's wheelchair in front of the door so that she couldn't leave without a final heart-wrenching embrace, Ginny reaching up from the chair, bawling, tears and snot clogging her beautiful face, Vanessa comforting her, "Don't worry baby, your dad is gonna take care of you, everything is gonna be all right . . . I'll come to visit you . . . If he lets me."

In the thirty or so seconds that she carried on with Ginny, my fury melted and Ginny's crying led to my own. We settled into a three-way sobbing hug after which I apologized for firing her, and Vanessa graciously accepted and agreed to stay on. For weeks after that incident I didn't dare to criticize when the bathwater was too hot or if she abandoned Ginny on the toilet for twenty minutes while she answered her cell phone messages. I played Mr. Everything-is-fine, but I was chewing the inside of my cheeks raw. I would fire her but not until I had a replacement. The next time it wouldn't be an angry outburst, just short and sweet, "So long, Vanessa, we won't be needing you anymore. Your pay plus two weeks severance is in the envelope. Thank you for your help."

That was the daydream that I shared with Anita Mirai, Ginny's case manager at Independence Home Health. I had only met Anita once, when she made a home visit to determine our needs, but I phoned regularly with my complaints. There had been three aides before Vanessa, none of whom lasted more than a month, and Vanessa, for all our spats, was closing in on a year.

Anita knew that I wanted someone better, but she reminded me of reality. "I am always looking out for you, but these are the pools of people who are applying for our jobs. We are not IBM." Anita was an RN who had managerial skills as well. She told me that she had worked as an aide herself while she was a student and getting accustomed to America, so different from Mumbai. "There are always difficulties working in the home. The home is not a neutral environment for the aide, and in your case we have the extra difficulty of Ginny not being able to speak, so you must communicate for her."

"Not so," I said, "Ginny uses her talker very well. I need someone who will show up on time and pay attention to my daughter for five hours. How hard is that?"

"I pointed out to you," Anita said, "that most aides are wanting eight hours daily plus the possibility of overtime. But I am always keeping you and Ginny in mind."

Carol kept us in mind, too, and though nobody really believed me when I said so, I bore my ex-wife very little ill will. People thought our marriage ended because of the stress of raising a handicapped child, but in fact Carol and I both knew that Ginny kept us together years longer than we might otherwise have stayed married. We became a solid team caring for Ginny, planning her school and medical needs, and we both learned to adjust our expectations. We didn't think about living happily ever after. We learned how to do what we had to do every day without getting depressed, because Ginny really was a beautiful and intelligent girl who seemed happy in spite of all the things that she couldn't do. And we adjusted our expectations of one another as well, gradually, so that by the end we were still solid co-workers in our daughter's care, a job that required trust but could be done without love.

At work, Carol soared. She had always been a math whiz, and when BankAmerica moved her from mortgages to derivatives and futures she did so spectacularly well that the bank decided they needed her in New York. That was when we finally called off the marriage. I had known about Scott from the start; in fact, I might have known before he did because, one thing about Carol, she gets right to the point. A few hours after Ginny's birth, when we heard the news of our child's brain damage from a group of four doctors, Carol stayed in control. When she saw that she couldn't hold back tears, she asked for pen and paper and wrote out the most important question: "What is the prognosis for her intelligence?"

When it came to our marriage she was just as direct. We had just put Ginny to bed. "I don't think you've noticed," she said, "but I haven't been myself lately—I'm distracted. I find it hard to concentrate. It's so troublesome that I've had to analyze why this is happening to me." She unfolded her arms as if she was about to hand me the answer. Carol doesn't try to look beautiful but men notice her. She's slim, wears her light brown hair short, what she calls a boy cut, and the whole package, her seriousness and the way she's not trying to seduce, really does. "There is a man," she said, "Scott Rogers, he works in commercial loans, I've known for some time that he's interested. He flirts," she gave an embarrassed laugh. "I don't respond, it's frankly annoying, but I do like him. I've told him a lot about Ginny and about us."

"Are you asking my permission?"

"No," she said, "I've already decided to go ahead with him, but before I even start, I want you to know that everything else will be the same. Ginny needs both of us."

After she told me, I stopped talking to her unless it was something about Ginny. We lived that way for about a month until I couldn't take it anymore and asked for a truce. She hugged me and I didn't push her away.

"I don't blame you a bit," she said, "I know how hard this is, but we need a plan for the future. I think you'll feel better if we come up with something."

What we came up with was pretty straightforward. After Ginny went to bed, Carol would go directly to Scott's condominium, and return at 6:30 the next morning, in time to wake Ginny and help get her ready for school. Usually Ginny slept through the night, but if there was a problem, Carol promised to be at her bedside within fifteen minutes of hearing from me.

Pretty quickly I realized that by getting up a half hour early I could handle the morning routine without Carol. I could get myself ready then feed and dress Ginny, put her on the school bus, and still make it to my job at Allen Middle School before the bell. I preferred rushing myself a little to seeing Carol right after she'd left Scott's house.

By the time we started this new schedule I had already met him. Scott was tall, looked athletic and tan, and seemed very aloof, always looking toward the distance. I was jealous and barely civil at first. But this rangy, confident banker was hardly what he seemed. He looked toward the horizon so much because he had an eye disease that made it hard for him to focus; and the tan—that came indirectly from asthma and a chronic sinus infection that responded best to a sunlamp. And at night Scott told me he used a face mask and a pump that forced oxygen to keep him from dying of sleep apnea. He looked like a lifeguard, but he was really more like a hypochondriac.

And he was honest. He told Carol right off that he liked Ginny and didn't mind spending a lot of hours with her, but he couldn't take on that sort of responsibility full time. This accounted for our year in limbo—he couldn't take on Ginny and Carol couldn't leave her. Then, once the bank put the squeeze on, Carol decided that she could move but only if I agreed to the move. We worked out our divorce in less than a week. I didn't even use a lawyer. Carol wanted to pay double what any court would have ordered in child support, and she gave me the house outright. "I want you to have a life, too," she said, "a good life. You deserve it." She was always sending me gifts from New York, cashmere sweaters from Saks, a thousand-dollar check for my birthday, and more clothes and toys than five Ginnys could use. So, even though she was now married to Scott I almost considered her my wife too, because I spoke to her daily and she was still helping me raise our child in every way that she could.

But even if it seemed like I had a wife at a distance, what I really had up close was a home health aide. My three pre-Vanessa helpers seemed to have come to our house directly from the ten o'clock local news. Marquita left, understandably, because her house burned down; fire set by her fourteen-year-old son. Yolanda's mother's boyfriend raped her, and Loretta got a staph infection from the needles that an artist used to tattoo her children's names onto her right forearm. After those three, Vanessa seemed like a gift from the middle class. She owned a car, had a steady boyfriend, and her thirteen-year-old son, Lamont, was an honor student at Parker school. She was thirty and reminded me of Lena Horne, the jazz singer my parents had admired, and as I learned bits and pieces about her past, it turned out that Vanessa had, in fact, worked at the fringes of the entertainment industry. She had been a dancer at a club, a singing waitress, and a hostess with a band that specialized in bar mitzvahs. Her job, to lure the shy twelve- and thirteen-year-olds onto the dance floor, where she taught them the latest steps.

"But I gave that stuff up," Vanessa told me, "because it was just getting to me. I was like some kind of wind up let's-be-happy doll, so I decided to go to nursing school to help people, mostly kids."

Nursing school meant four weeks at the Allied Academy for an associates degree, but that was four weeks more training than any of the others had. Fortunately, Ginny didn't need nursing, just someone to feed her, bathe her, help with second-grade homework, and, most of all, just be there.

Vanessa brought a lot of music to the house, hip-hop, Power 99 radio, which I wasn't crazy about, but Ginny was too young to understand the sexual lyrics and she really loved moving her hands to the rhythms, which she called dancing. I allowed the radio while Vanessa helped Ginny with the leg lifts and stretches that the physical therapist wanted her to do every day.

The other exercises, the ones for oral motor therapy, I did those with Ginny because I thought they were too important to delegate. Ginny could make sounds and she liked to "talk," but she couldn't shape her sounds into words. She could say a lot of things on her electronic talker but it took a long time, and especially when she was with children it was hard because they didn't want to wait the minute or more that it might take her to tap out "May I play with you?"

For a half-hour every day Ginny and I used a deck of special cards, each one picturing Oral Motor Mary, a Raggedy Ann type who kept her mouth wide open at all times. Every card had instructions for a particular exercise: "Pretend that the tip of your tongue is looking for a treasure that is buried under your left rear molar. Not there? Then why not try the right one?"

Because I couldn't stop myself, I did all the exercises with Ginny so that at the end of our half hour sessions I felt as if my mouth had been doing push-ups. For me, of course, it was easy to manipulate the tongue, but for Ginny it was as hard as if those cards directed her to reposition her kidneys or liver. Once a week we went to Children's Hospital for a new stack of exercise cards and some encouragement from Sharon, the oral motor therapist.

Sharon always started Ginny with a snack. "Eating is the best tongue exercise, isn't it?" Sharon stayed upbeat and even in the clinical environment, casual. The others in her office wore white medical jackets, Sharon wore blue jeans and sandals. After the snack she would show Ginny pictures of her own children, "Hal" and "Sue." Their real names were Rudy and Mary Kay, which were too hard, so she made up the nicknames. "Sometimes we even use those nicknames at home," she told Ginny. "Thank you for giving us such a good idea."

Sharon believed in setting specific vocal goals. "It's not going to be quick and it's not going to be pretty, but we're going to make progress. A word here and there can make such a difference."

Ginny didn't need yes and no, because she could shake her head. And she could raise her hand, the universal sign for the bathroom. "Let's pick an everyday word for our goal," Sharon suggested. "How about . . ." She looked at me. "How about Pa Pa?" Sharon made it into two words with a deep breath in between each vocalization of the explosive p. Ginny smiled and nodded. "Pa Pa" became her goal. At every session after trying to blow strips of Kleenex and working at getting a sound out of a kazoo and lying on a mat for ten minutes of attempted yoga breathing, Ginny ended each session by pursing her lips and flattening her tongue for an attempt at "Pa Pa."

Things were going along pretty well in daily life, I thought, until Kate Sanborn, the 7A teacher, invited me to a Rockets basketball game. "I've got fantastic seats," she said, "not just tickets, courtside, second row." Her brother, she told me, worked now and then for the Rockets on legal matters and he got her the tickets. Everyone at Allen Middle School knew that I was a big fan. Last year's fifth-graders pooled their gift money to buy me a ball autographed by the entire Rockets team. I kept it on a little stand on my desk at school to remind me not so much of the Rockets but of how much I liked that particular group of fifth graders.

Ginny never wanted me to go out at night, but I had to from time to time for parent meetings and other school events, and sometimes just to go to the movies or to break the routine by having dinner out. I always prepared her a day or two in advance, and as long as it was Vanessa and not a stranger putting her to bed, there were no problems. I was trying to teach Ginny basketball so we could watch together on TV, but she was too young to show much interest.

On that Thursday of the Rockets-Lakers game, when Vanessa didn't show up to meet the bus, I rushed out of school fifteen minutes early. Eddie, the bus driver, was standing in front of the house beside Ginny's wheelchair. "I hated to call you at work, Jack," he said. "When Vanessa's just a few minutes late I take the other kids home and then circle back, but I've been waiting here a half hour and I've got to get home, too."

I thanked him and apologized and then I started trying to reach Vanessa on her cell phone and her home phone. I was supposed to pick up Kate at 6:30 for a 7:30 tip-off. I waited until 6:20 hoping Vanessa would show up or at least call, but finally I had to let Kate know that I couldn't make it.

"Oh no," she said, then she caught herself, and I could visualize her staying calm, even forcing a smile the way she did at school, being a good citizen about her disappointment.

"These things happen," she said, "there will be other games."

"Sure," I said, because I was feeling too bitter to really say anything.

The next day I left school early to meet the bus at 3:15 and there was Vanessa, her hair done up in cornrows and decorated with colorful ribbons.

"I'm sorry," she said, "but I was just sick as a dog yesterday. That allergy came down on me like it was gonna choke me to death. You remember when I ate that half of a banana, not even a half and I got so swelled up that you wanted to call me an ambulance."

"I remember," I said, "and I was going to call Dr. Portnoy, who lives down the block, not an ambulance. And you were better in a half-hour."

"Not last night I wasn't. I really thought that was gonna be the end."

"But I see that you were still able to get your hair done. Was it supposed to be for your funeral?"

"There you go getting nasty," she said, "no calling for that. I'm sorry you missed your old game, but when a person's sick is there some law against doing something to make yourself feel better?"

"Were you too sick to call, too?"

"You can just take that one up with Verizon. I'm one week late on the bill, and they go cuttin' me off with no notice. I'm gonna give them something, treating me like that when I've been a customer for three years and their hitting me up for extra minutes every month that I know I don't owe them."

I got into my Honda and drove back to school because I didn't want to listen to any more excuses. I called the agency to complain and Anita confirmed that Vanessa had in fact called in sick, but not until 10 PM, and by then they thought it was beside the point to inform me that she wasn't coming to work.

I had lunch-hour shift with Kate the next day, and she seemed perky and ready to forget the basketball game, but I knew that was just the way she was. It was Kate I took to the movies and sometimes out to dinner, but I told her that I wouldn't be getting married, not for a good long time, if ever. Sometimes we had sex like teenagers in the car because I had to get home quickly, and sometimes we spent a few hours together at her apartment. Kate was closing in on forty and had moved every few years from one district middle school to another because of a failed romance. "This time," she said, "I'm not running away." She'd been at Allen for three years and the staff adored her. She never forgot birthdays, and she was the one who took over your class in an emergency, just moving her own kids in like a twenty-person help crew.

I was the only eligible male at school, and I understood that everyone was rooting for Kate to snag me. I was, too. I wished that I could feel as sweaty and nervous and excited with Kate as I felt at Children's Hospital while I watched Ginny struggle to get her lips to purse and her tongue to flatten and her lungs to exhale, all in coordination so that she could say "Pa Pa," her goal and mine, too.

Every once in a while a word or a phrase did happen, without practice or plan. Once Sharon and I both heard "I wanna go," right after snack. Ginny just beamed when we understood the words, as she had every right to, and Sharon and I hugged each other. But most of the time it was just grunting into the tape recorder; followed by the attempts to blow out a birthday candle and move the tissue strip and then the Oral Motor Mary review. Insurance-documented work, the slow frustrating attempts to overcome the loss at birth of ten or twenty million neurons. Ginny never complained, never said that it was time to give up. She worked so hard at speech because she wanted the most human thing, words, and I never doubted how much she had to say.

Before we split up, Carol and I had been planning for two years to take Ginny to Disneyland, but something always came up. We canceled one trip when Ginny's food went down the wrong way and caused aspiration pneumonia. The second cancellation came right after I'd learned about Scott, and I refused to go because I didn't want to spend a weekend in the hotel with Carol. Then there was the cancellation when Scott and Carol were planning to take Ginny but Scott had a panic attack, which caused his asthma to kick in.

Finally, in the sweet aftermath of signing our divorce decree, when we both felt such relief, and when Carol's generosity and love for me were on display more than they had been for years, she said, "Why don't you take Ginny to Disneyland next weekend, her first weekend without me. I think it will be a good start on her new life."

I agreed and we had a great time. No waiting in line, not for kids in wheelchairs. On the first day we climbed Space Mountain, visited

Tomorrowland, took two semichilling roller coasters, and there was always a helpful employee nearby to meet us with the chair at the exit point. We had a weekend of nonstop fun with Mickey and the gang, and on our last afternoon, when we visited Minnie's house, all the characters came over to greet the sweet little girl in the wheelchair, Minnie and Goofy and Pinocchio crowded around, and suddenly it occurred to me that for the first time in her life Ginny was surrounded by people like her, people who couldn't talk. Minnie made elaborate hand gestures of welcome and clasped her hands to her heart to signal affection. She seated us at one of her parlor tables and let us know by the pathos in her folded hands that if she were allowed by company rules to serve tea or anything else she would bring it out in no time. She and her friends wore large heads, but apparently lightweight ones because the heads didn't seem to be a burden to them. Goofy escorted us quietly into the living room, and then, on the porch, when we were almost at the exit to Minnie's house, Ginny broke the silence. She tapped out slowly on her talker to a very surprised Pinocchio, "Have you wife?" The character read the question on her computer screen and his large face, of course, remained fixed, but he did move his head from side to side.

I thought of Minnie and her silent companions sometimes when Ginny and I walked to the farmers market. We did this to fill our Saturday mornings, which had always been Carol's time when they did mother-daughter things like braiding Ginny's hair or baking lemon squares. Our route to the outdoor market took us through a few blocks of abandoned houses and shops. It wasn't dangerous, the police kept a pretty close watch on things, but you couldn't avoid the homeless people who had taken over the sidewalks.

Ginny, in her purple Quicky wheelchair and with her blond curls, must have looked like the Faerie Queene to them. But the fascination was mutual. The two or three bag ladies, the men in the doorways, accustomed to being stared at themselves, watched our every move, and Ginny stared back at them, just as she had stared at the Disney characters. Because we walked through almost every Saturday morning, the regulars began to recognize us. With nothing better to do, they waited for Ginny. Some of them called out to her, nothing unusual, nice things like "Hi there, sweetheart" or "How are you doing, cutie," harmless greetings, and I didn't object until one of the ladies tried to offer Ginny jewelry, a copper bracelet. She took it off her own blue black wrist. Before she could get it on to Ginny's arm I stopped her. "Please," I said, "she really has so many bracelets."

"This is a healing one," the woman said. Even though it must have been 80 she was wearing a wool hat and sweater, and gloves that covered half of each finger. I could smell the urine on her clothes, and I didn't want her to touch Ginny.

"Let her wear this," she said, pushing my arm aside. "I couldn't move my left wrist, and this bracelet cured me."

"Then for sure we won't take it," I said, "You keep it and stay well. And honestly, my daughter has so much jewelry. But if the copper has helped you, I'll try to get one for her, just like yours."

"It's not the copper," she said, "this is a healing bracelet. It's blessed by Jesus Christ, and he wants her to walk." We stayed in a small struggle over access to Ginny's hand until finally I turned the wheelchair around and walked in the other direction, ready to give up the farmers market if we had to, but the woman followed us.

"I'm not gonna hurt her," she said, "just take this—from Jesus."

I let her slip the bracelet over Ginny's wrist. Later I would throw it away and scrub my daughter's arm. I tried to hurry through that block, but Ginny began punching at her talker with her left forefinger as she always does. The bag lady followed us and watched in fascination as she saw the squares of the electronic device begin to light up.

"Do you see that? Now she can use her arm."

"She could always use her arm," I said, "that's how she talks—her finger hits the squares of the talker and she constructs sentences that way." The woman leaned her face over Ginny's shoulder so that she could read the screen.

"Give money," Ginny's talker said. I had forgotten to lower the volume on the machine so the robotic voice blared out her message for all to hear. I handed the woman a dollar, which she refused to take, so I gave it and whatever change I had in my pocket to the onlookers.

A toothless man whom I recognized from previous walks came over to escort us as if he was a private security guard. He took the bag lady's arm and led her away so that we could pass by without being harassed further. I didn't try to stop him when he put his arm around me. He walked with us as if he and I were old buddies, fellow soldiers fighting the good fight. I gave him a dollar when we reached the farmers market. "Feed your girl honey," he advised, "good clover honey."

We only stayed a little while at the market that Saturday, and I decided to avoid the street people by taking the long way home, really over a mile extra, and a lot of it uphill, a long distance to push the wheelchair, especially when I was holding a few bags of fruits and vegetables.

When we got home Vanessa was on the porch waiting for us, even though she didn't work on Saturdays. She noticed the copper bracelet right away, so I told her how Ginny got it.

"I really hate the way they think that Ginny is one of them, as if all unfortunates are the same."

"Ain't they?" Vanessa asked.

"No, Ginny is not responsible for what happened to her. They are. They're adults, they've had lives, they didn't have to end up in the shape they're in."

"How you know that?" Vanessa said. "You don't know them."

"They've got arms and legs and voices, nobody has to live that way. Here," I said, "maybe you want this bracelet, it's blessed by Jesus." Usually Vanessa didn't take offense at my tendency to moralize but I had picked the wrong moment.

"How you teach the fifth graders anything when you don't understand nothing yourself." She put her head down on the breakfast bar. Without looking up she said, "That motherfucker Jason just threw me out, he must have had his new woman for a long time and was just looking for a chance to get rid of me." Vanessa was dressed beautifully in a purple silk pantsuit but there were no ribbons in her hair rows.

"Please," I said, "let's not discuss this now." I nodded toward Ginny.

"I'm sorry," she said. "It's okay, honey, Vanessa's gonna be fine. Just a little problem now so I came over to see you, is that okay, can Vanessa play here for a while?"

"Of course," I said.

As soon as I put Ginny down for her nap I started getting the dinner ingredients spread out on the kitchen counter. I had invited Kate. She had met Ginny several times, but I'd never had her over for dinner, mostly because it was easier to go out or to go to her house, where we could do more than eat together. I wanted to do something special to make up for the missed game. It turned out that her brother's tickets weren't free. She had paid $320 for the pair. A dinner wouldn't cover that but I wanted to let her know that I understood the effort she had made to please me. And I thought this was as good a time as any for Kate to see my life as a father up close. I was planning to cook Chinese in the electric wok so there wasn't much preparation, only chopping. I didn't want Vanessa around, especially today, but I couldn't send her away when I wasn't sure she knew where she would be going.

"Do you have a plan?" I asked. She shook her head.

"What about your sister?" Vanessa rolled her eyes. "She's got five kids and anyway half the time she's doin' crack."

''What about friends? . . . Just for a few days until you can get your bearings."

"My friends are like me," she said, "or worse off."

There was no attitude in Vanessa now. Her hand shook the cup as she sipped the green tea that I knew she liked.

"I feel ashamed," she said, "I don't like you seeing me like this."

"What about Lamont?" I asked.

"He's been with his dad in Georgia since September. He's been going to school there all this year. They done him bad at Parker."

"I thought . . ."

"You thought wrong."

I explained that I had a guest coming for dinner at seven.

"Your girlfriend?" she asked.

"Yes," I said, "I guess you could say that."

"Can I stay and help with Ginny? That way you can talk and whatever."

"Of course you can," I said, "but what about after that?"

"I'll think of something," she said. And she did. While Kate Sanborn was in the living room going over with Ginny the directions to *Who Said What?*, the game that she had brought as a gift, Vanessa approached me in the kitchen. I had just put the rice into a serving bowl and she held up for my approval the fruit platter that she had cut for dessert. I was checking the pineapple for any signs of rind.

"If I was white, would you have been coming on to me?"

"What are you talking about?"

"You know what I'm talking about. You're always going on about the schoolteacher and the therapist and your great old wife, and it's me here everyday—me—helpin' you raise the child. A man and a woman. It don't take too much figuring."

She put the fruit plate on the counter and glared at me, as if she was identifying the criminal in a courtroom.

"I don't know what you're getting at," I said. "Your job is to help Ginny. That's it. I think you know that I appreciate all the help you've given her."

"You think that schoolteacher is gonna do as good as I do?"

"I've got a guest, Vanessa, you're welcome to stay for dinner. If you'd rather not, fine. And if you want to talk about things that are bothering you, this isn't the time."

She didn't storm out and seemed to calm down, but I still asked her to sit across the table so that I could feed Ginny instead of letting her do it. I didn't think that Kate noticed any tension as we talked about basketball and Chinese food and Allen Middle School. When Vanessa stayed after the meal to join us for a game of *Who Said What?* I thought her burst of anger was over. But when it was her turn to question someone she asked Ginny, "Who would you rather have taking care of you, me or her?"

Kate blushed to her hair roots. I tried to stay calm. "That's not a fair question, Vanessa, please think of something else."

"That's the only question I've got."

"Please excuse Vanessa," I said to Kate, although I was looking at the aide. "Vanessa's in the midst of a personal crisis that has nothing to do with us. She's not herself."

"That's true," Vanessa said. She reached over to hold Ginny's hand. "I'm sorry, girlfriend," she said.

I hadn't paid attention to Ginny while I focused on Vanessa and Kate so I didn't observe my daughter as she inhaled and then pursed her lips and flattened her tongue and coordinated all the movements that produced the word.

"Ma Ma," she said, letting us know in a clear, strong voice her goal.

The Jew of Home Depot

THE OLD MAN in Marshall, Texas, phoned the Chabad organization in August 1980. He got right to the point. "I'm eighty-five and dying," Jerome Baumgarten said, "and I'm surrounded by Gentiles. If you can send me a bunch of real Jews, I'll pay their way and make it worth their while."

When the director of the special projects office offered the performance of this good deed to Reb Avram Hirsch and his family of eight daughters and one son, Reb Avram accepted without hesitation. His wife, Malka, and the Hirsch children packed hurriedly, as if in an emergency. They didn't disconnect the cooking gas or the telephone line and the younger girls, none of whom had traveled beyond New Jersey, were excited to be on an airplane, and after that on a Greyhound bus, all on the same day.

In the lobby of the Hotel Marshall their benefactor awaited them in a green velvet chair. He wore both suspenders and a belt, which flapped against his shrunken waist. The family stood before him as if he was their commanding officer. Mr. Baumgarten raised himself from the chair unaided, although a bellman stood close by and at the ready.

"Shalom," Mr. Baumgarten called out. He pointed out the flag of the Republic of Texas on the pole next to the American flag and then he looked carefully at the family. "Are all these children from the same mother?" he asked.

"Thanks to God," Reb Avram said.

Chaim, the eighteen-year-old son, noticed that their benefactor wore garters on his shirtsleeves, making the sleeves puff out at the elbows. The girls whispered to one another in Yiddish that Mr. Baumgarten was so skinny and the waistband of his trousers so large that he looked like a straw standing in a glass of milk. He had a full head of white hair and a voice that treated everyone as if they were more deaf than himself. He introduced the family to Ed Sanders at the registration desk, and to Eural, the bellman.

"You all can take over my house," Mr. Baumgarten told the Hirsches. "I've moved into the hotel because it's close to the hospital and the undertaker and here I can get what I want if I bribe this old colored man enough." The bellman laughed. "Yes sir, he's mister big tipper," Eural said.

"Pay no attention to him," Jerome Baumgarten said. "Eural knows the dollar bill in his hand, but human suffering—that's nothing to him, nothing to any of them." He waved his hand at the hotel lobby. "They're all happy to die and come home to Jesus. But I'm sitting here facing forever and I don't know anything about it. That's why I asked for you, for pious Jews, for my own kind to be with me now."

Reb Avram moved closer to Mr. Baumgarten, "Do you know the Hasidic song, the whole world is a narrow bridge and the most important thing is not to be afraid?"

"Never heard of it," Mr. Baumgarten said. Reb Avram began to sing the Bratislav melody and his family joined him.

"I am afraid, that's true enough." Mr. Baumgarten said, "but I don't understand that language." The Hirsches stopped singing. "My family and I are here to help you, you won't be alone," Reb Avram said.

"Good," Jerome Baumgarten said. "But I've never been much for singing."

When the family left the hotel, Eural, who seemed almost as old as Mr. Baumgarten, led them to their temporary home. The Hirsches followed him along Main Street four blocks beyond what Eural said was the college, to Fraternity Row, a street of three-story houses, each one labeled at the front with Greek letters. Eural stopped in front of a white Victorian with a wraparound porch and balcony. "Mr. Baumgarten's house is the only private one, the rest is all Greeks," he said.

The family stood in front of the house not daring to follow Eural as he climbed the porch steps and then unlocked the front door. He waved for them to follow him. Reb Avram went first. He took a mezuzah from his pocket, applied Velcro to its back and mounted it on the door post. He kissed the mezuzah with his fingers then nodded for the rest of his family to follow him into their new quarters. "There's a lot of house here," the bellman said.

"I can't believe it's all for us," Malka said. "In Brooklyn five families could live in a house like this." They entered slowly, the children speaking in whispers as if they were in a library or museum. They touched the oak paneling of the living room walls; they checked the bottoms of their shoes to be certain that they weren't marking the polished wood floors or staining the Persian carpets. Only on the upper floors did the Hirsch girls speak aloud, claiming bedrooms for themselves, flushing toilets, looking for secret passages. The girls and their parents took the five bedrooms, Chaim had to himself the entire third floor. And it was there, while looking through a window in the attic of Mr. Baumgarten's house on his first night in Marshall, Texas, that Chaim saw the forbidden.

At first he thought it was fantasy, a vision of bleached bones like the prophet Ezekiel had seen. Chaim turned his back to the window he had opened to let fresh air into the musty attic bedroom. As he pulled the window closed, he heard her name, Laura. Then he sat down on the thin mattress and watched her. He tried to think of holy things, the parting of the Red Sea and the wonderous burning bush, but even as his mind conjured up the sacred fire, his eyes took in the form of the beautiful shiksa, Laura, across the driveway with a man in the Phi Kappa Delta house. Revulsion filled his soul, but as she played the harlot, Chaim watched.

The next morning he went to his father just as Reb Avram was hurrying to leave for the hotel, where he had already begun to instruct their patron in Jewish law and custom. Chaim, like his father, stood over six feet tall and had a light complexion and reddish hair. Mr. Baumgarten had been surprised by their appearance and size. "I expected undernourished types like I see on the calendar pictures," he told Reb Avram, "but you and your son look like linebackers."

"Father, I'd like to return home," Chaim said.

Reb Avram opened his hands in wonder. "The second day here and already you want to go home? I would expect this from Feigele, from a three-year-old, but not from you."

"I'm not comfortable," Chaim said, "please . . ."

"You're not comfortable for a day or two, but think of Mr. Baumgarten who has not been comfortable for eighty-some years, who has never had a minyan, or kosher food, or any Jewish learning. Think of him and maybe you'll become comfortable."

"I'm trying," Chaim said.

"Try more," Reb Avram said.

Chaim knew, of course, about what happened between men and women. Even before his bar mitzvah, his father had instructed him and they had studied together the laws of female purity. At that time Reb Avram had pointed out exactly why a pious man wears a ritual belt around his midsection. "Those things that happen below, those are the ways that a man is like an animal, so we mark the difference by wearing a belt. Animal below the waist, but the image of God above."

At the age of thirteen Chaim began wearing a black string belt but only during his waking hours. Now that he needed to be reminded that he was created in the image of Hashem he kept it on at night as well. From his tiny window, like those he had seen in pictures of sailing ships, he looked directly into the room of one of the brothers of Phi Kappa Delta. On the walls in the room across the driveway Chaim saw photos of movie stars and football players. These distractions did not affect him, nor did the music and the occasional yelling that came from the fraternity. Brooklyn had accustomed him to noise.

On his second night in Texas he was waiting for her when she sat down at the desk near the window, placed some schoolbooks beside her, and began to read. In a few minutes a young man entered the room and handed her a bottle of beer. Chaim winced as she put it to her lips. He wished that she had used a glass. She put the bottle down and returned to her book. This pleased him. He wanted to think of her as a serious student. And if the young man wanted to study sitting next to her or across from her desk, that would also be good. The man left the room and while he was gone, Chaim enjoyed being alone with her. She read so diligently that Chaim wondered what the book was about. Then the man came back into the room, Laura turned from the book, and Chaim lost all his sense of boundaries. He could close his eyes but only for a few seconds, and when he didn't watch there was no relief because he imagined even more than he was seeing.

Later, Laura returned to the desk and to her book as if nothing had happened. Later still she walked downstairs and out of the fraternity house and he could hear her start her car and drive away. It was past 2 AM but sleep no longer meant anything to Chaim Hirsch.

While Chaim suffered in private from his family's hasty journey to Texas, his mother worried openly about the situation of Mindel, the firstborn Hirsch, also a redhead and like a second mother to her sisters. Mindel had received a marriage proposal from Yossi Goodman, an eye doctor from the Bensonhurst neighborhood. Mindel had returned from meeting her prospective mate at the Kennedy airport passenger lounge to tell her mother and waiting sisters that Dr. Goodman said that he was ready for the next step. But when Reb Avram met the eye doctor, he withheld his permission. "I've heard that three girls have already turned him down," Reb Avram said. "There must be something that's not right, let's wait until I find out more."

"Maybe there's something wrong with those girls, not him," Mindel said. "I like Dr. Goodman, father. I'm sure he'll be a good husband to me."

"Maybe so, but a little later you can still like him. There doesn't have to be such a hurry, the man is thirty-three years old, and you're nineteen. That's also something to think about." Then, while Reb Avram was still considering the match for his firstborn, the sudden move to Texas put the eye doctor on the back burner.

Mindel reluctantly accompanied her family to Texas, but she took no interest in their new surroundings. While the younger girls made themselves at home in Mr. Baumgarten's linen closet and traded bedcoverings, while they helped their mother boil cutlery and chop vegetables, Mindel liked to walk through the town, imagining herself a young matron on her way to a certain eye doctor's office. Late in the day, after she had finished washing the dinner plates, she liked to sit on the front porch the way people did on much smaller porches in Crown Heights. As she daydreamed of her future, the fraternity boys who passed by, to a man, treated Mindel with respect. They called her "sister." Some attempted to bow and others put their hands together as if they were praying rather than greeting a neighbor.

"They're so polite to my face," she told her mother "and then at night they scream and drink beer. What's the matter with them?" Malka urged her daughter to ignore their neighbors. "We'll only be here for a few weeks. When its his time, Mr. Baumgarten, I hope without suffering, will go to the next world, and then, when we're home, your Dr. Goodman will come to the house. He'll talk to your father again, and everything will be all right. You'll see."

Among the Hirsches, only Malka, thin and worried, looked the role of the ghetto mother. She herself marveled sometimes, as she said a prayer against the evil eye, at her son and those tall slim light-haired beauties, her daughters, who waited patiently along with her for the death of Jerome Baumgarten.

For their first Shabbat in Marshall, Reb Avram awoke before dawn on Friday morning and at the local farmers market bought four plump chickens. With Chaim's help he hung them upside down from a low branch in Mr. Baumgarten's spacious backyard and slit their throats according to the laws of kashrut. Behind the fence that separated the Hirsch family from the Phi Kappa Delta house, several fraternity brothers watched the ritual slaughter in silence. The girls picked the feathers from the carcasses and then helped their mother clean the house and cook for the Sabbath meal.

Just before sunset, with all the Hirsches assembled on the porch overlooking Fraternity Row, Mr. Baumgarten arrived. He drove his own car and parked the white Cadillac without difficulty, then he invited everyone to the curb to have a look at his custom interior. He allowed the girls to run their fingers over the saddle leather seats engraved like branded cattle with a letter *B* in a circle. "That upholstery is a stupid waste of money, I know it. And so is a Caddy," Mr. Baumgarten said. "But when a person is alone and he has no heirs, and he is surrounded by car dealers and ranchers, this is what can happen to him."

As they lit the candles and all the girls stood before him scrubbed for the Sabbath queen, and as the older ones rose to help their mother serve or to attend to their little sisters, Mr. Baumgarten said, "I sold diamonds all my life, Reb Hirsch, but you have created diamonds."

After dinner they surprised their benefactor. The family had left his room, the master bedroom on the first floor, untouched. Malka assured Mr. Baumgarten that he would no longer have to spend the Sabbath alone at the hotel. Every Friday evening he could return to his own room with his familiar Oriental carpet, his mahogany bed and matching desk, his closet of size forty short-portly suits, his custom-made size 7½ hand tooled boots. Mr. Baumgarten seemed surprised and deeply touched. "Don't be silly," he said, "go ahead, use the room for yourselves. I intended for you to use the whole house. For one night a week what does it matter where I sleep? Stick me under the stairwell or in the closet, what more do I need?"

Chana Tobka, the seven-year-old, the one with the mouth on her, said to her mother while Mr. Baumgarten listened, "Why don't we let him sleep in the closet? I want to try his hot tub." Mr. Baumgarten smiled at her wickedness, but Reb Avram burned his daughter with his eyes. "Never speak like that again," he said. "That is forbidden language, that is *loshen hora*. Do you hear me? We are in this house and in this city for one reason, for the sake of Mr. Baumgarten. God forbid that he who is giving us so much should be forced out of his own room."

When the Hirsch family gathered in the living room to sing Sabbath hymns, Mr. Baumgarten tried to hum along with the choral repetitions. "Is this what it will be like in the world to come, will the souls spend all day and all night and all of forever singing?"

"About the next world nobody knows for sure," Reb Avram said. "But the rabbis tell us that the Lord's Tisch, his Sabbath table, is as long as the distance from the earth to the moon, and there is a seat for everyone that has ever lived. And Hashem sits there, so far removed that none can see him, but everyone feels his presence as if he is right beside you handing you a spoon to taste your soup to see if it's not too hot."

"And will I be sitting at that Tisch?" Mr. Baumgarten asked. "Don't you have to be a saint to be that close to the Lord?"

"Of course not," Reb Avram said. "There are no saints, we don't believe in saints. All people make mistakes."

"You bet we make mistakes," Mr. Baumgarten said. "When there are so many rules like in the IRS regulations or city ordinances or blue laws and sales tax rules. I'll bet that there are probably more rules in the tax code than in the whole Torah. No person can dot every last *i* or have an accountant or rabbi for every question that comes up in the course of the day, can he?"

"Hashem is merciful," Reb Avram said.

"I hope so," Mr. Baumgarten said, "I sure hope so. It only seems right, doesn't it?"

Reb Avram agreed. He would have preferred to discuss such speculative things in the hotel privately with Mr. Baumgarten instead of in front of his family, but he enjoyed seeing the pleasure that the old man took in hearing cabalistic myths about the next world.

"You know what I'll say if I'm at that table," Mr. Baumgarten announced, "I'll say that I'm the son of a Lithuanian peddler who settled in Yell County, and thought that Arkansas was already heaven. And now here I am at the right hand of the Lord. Hard to believe, isn't it?"

The assembled Hirsch family all disagreed—it was not hard to believe. "When I was a young man," Jerome Baumgarten said, allowing his mind to wander, "when my father settled in Arkansas, nobody paid much attention to things down there except for Franklin Delano Roosevelt. He came to the Hot Springs because the water helped his legs. I suppose that Franklin Roosevelt's sitting at the Lord's table, probably all the important dead people are."

"You don't have to be important," Reb Avram said. "How important you are in this world doesn't matter. The man who sells pencils and shoelaces on the street corner, in the world to come he can be just as important as the president."

Before Mr. Baumgarten retired for the night, Reb Avram and Malka assembled the children and reintroduced them by name from youngest to oldest. When Reb Avram presented Mindel, to her surprise, her father told Mr. Baumgarten that she had a proposal of marriage. Mindel blushed to her ears. Mr. Baumgarten scratched his own right ear with his car key. "No surprise there," he said. "She's a beautiful girl. Is the man one of your people, I mean is he one of the pious?"

"Yes," Reb Avram said, "we wouldn't consider someone who wasn't. But I have some questions about this man . . ."

"Father, please," Mindel said. "Goodnight, Mr. Baumgarten." She left the room holding back tears as Miriam and Esther followed after her.

"She's upset because we moved away when everything was still up in the air about her marriage," Reb Avram said.

"They're touchy at that stage, they all are, the men, too," Mr. Baumgarten said. "But I'm not one to complain about that, not when I've sold as many wedding ring sets as I have. What's the man's profession, if I may ask."

"He's an eye doctor, he has his own office," Reb Avram said.

"Optometrist or M.D.?"

"Optometrist, I think," Reb Avram said, "but I'm not really sure."

"Optometrist, that would be a quarter carat at most, that's my guess," Mr. Baumgarten said. "If he was a regular M.D., well, then you might be talking about a stone of some consequence."

Since the age of seven Chaim had been studying all day at a yeshiva. Sometimes he came home after everyone was asleep and ate alone and went off the next morning to study before the girls awoke for school. So, when he lost weight and his eyes darkened from lack of sleep, his sisters, not accustomed to seeing him, noticed nothing different about their brother, who, day by day, plotted a route around sin.

He moved his bed to the other side of the attic and then found himself at 1 AM sitting beside the window, his arms around his knees, rocking his body without any memory of having left his bed. At a pharmacy on Main Street he bought over-the-counter sleeping pills and tried one, and the next night two tablets, without relief or sleep. He threw the pills away, afraid that he might accidentally overdose. His death would be a relief, but he didn't want to embarrass his family, who would never be able to overcome such an incident. When he moved his bed back to the window, he considered it an act of finality as if he had been buried, and in that corner of the cemetery reserved for suicides and murderers.

Still, he tried to overcome the evil impulse. In the basement of the house Chaim found black fabric in an old steamer trunk. He carried the fabric and a roll of duct tape to the third floor. He doubled and redoubled the fabric until it was as thick as his hand, then he secured it to the brick wall with three layers of tape. That night, with his head beneath the blocked window, he saw nothing. The darkness was so severe that when he turned off his lamp it was as if, in punishment, Hashem had blinded him. Whenever he felt temptation, he recited the words of David the king who asked forgiveness after looking upon Bathsheba.

Have mercy upon me, O God, according to thy lovingkindness:
According to the multitude of thy tender mercies blot out my
transgressions.
Wash me thoroughly from mine iniquity,
And cleanse me from my sin.
For I know my transgressions;
And my sin is ever before me.

He repeated the psalm until he fell asleep, but after midnight, when on weekdays even Fraternity Row grew somewhat quiet, he was certain that he heard her voice. Chaim sat up and looked at the obstructed window, reciting again the words of King David over and over until the psalm felt lifeless on his tongue because neither the words nor the barrier he had constructed stopped his mind from lusting after what he could not see. He pulled at the duct tape until his knuckles bled. And when the layers of tape did not come away at once, he tore through the cloth. His bleeding fingers gripped the fabric and his breath clouded the window. He had abandoned the tree of life, the 613 commandments, and even the seven laws of decency from the time of Noah; all this so that he might look at Laura, her arms and legs visible in the moonlight, his pleasure as nothing compared to his shame.

Mr. Baumgarten had paid their travel expenses and had suggested to the Chabad officials and to Reb Avram himself that the Hirsch family would benefit immensely from his estate. But at the moment Reb Avram and Malka, after paying the deposit on the utility bill, had barely enough money for food. Reb Avram, nervous about asking for a stipend, arrived early at the hotel on Monday morning of their third week in Texas. He found Mr. Baumgarten in the hotel barbershop, his body tilted back, his face foamed, and Luther the barber examining the eminent man's face as if contemplating a sculpture. Mr. Baumgarten opened one eye to Reb Avram and raised a hand of greeting from beneath the barber's sheet.

"Tell the rabbi whose hair you cut, Luther." The barber looked up for a moment then returned his gaze to his customer. "Mr. Baumgarten brags on me too much," Luther said, "I'm just a small-town barber who had his one hour of fame."

"Come on Luther, tell him."

Without looking up from Mr. Baumgarten's cheek and chin, Luther said, "Over in Nam one time I cut the hair of Richard M. Nixon."

Mr. Baumgarten, only half shaved, raised himself. "He's got the hair of the thirty-eighth president of the United States of America." Mr. Baumgarten pointed to a jelly jar on the barber's comb shelf. "Think of it." Reb Avram shook his head. Jerome Baumgarten pointed again, "What's in that jar, that's about what a person leaves behind in this life. Am I right rabbi?"

Reb Avram nodded. He tried not to look directly at the jar of hair because it seemed like a pagan thing to keep it on display. He wished that he had waited in the lobby until Mr. Baumgarten had finished his haircut.

"Luther is a churchgoing man," Mr. Baumgarten said. "Most of the folks in Marshall are. You don't know how envious I've been all my life. I'd be sitting on my porch on a Sunday morning and watch them, families like yours rabbi, all dressed up and going to church. Luther's got, what is it, five kids?"

"Four," Luther said, "all grown up now."

"I'd watch everyone going off to church, and I would listen to the bells, and the town growing quieter and quieter, until you could almost feel that the Lord was holding all of Marshall in his hands, except for me, at home with the *Dallas Morning News* and a pot of coffee and wondering what a Jew does at such a time. What would you have done, rabbi?"

Reb Avram shook his head. "I don't know, maybe I would be praying myself."

"Well I guess that's what I did, too, sort of."

Once they were back in the hotel room, Reb Avram with much embarrassment mentioned the question of money. Jerome Baumgarten held up his hand like a stop sign. "Neither a borrower nor a lender be," he said.

"Yes, that's the best way, but we came immediately and without anything to surround you with yiddishkeit, to help you in your time of need."

"And I appreciate it, but my time of need isn't forty hours a week from eleven people. Why don't you and your family take advantage of your free time, rabbi, this is a gift not from Jerome Baumgarten, but from the Lord."

Reb Avram left with a check for five hundred dollars, one half of the funeral fee in advance, and with the understanding that he would not ask again. "No matter how my estate may benefit you in the long run, right now you need to become more self-sufficient. You're not doing your family any service by allowing them to wait around for a handout."

"Most of my family are only children," Reb Avram said.

"Even more important," Mr. Baumgarten said. "Childhood, that's where the bad habits begin."

Before he decided to act, Chaim walked four times to Home Depot without entering the building. On the fifth trip, he tried to pretend that he was looking for something. At the end of each aisle he stopped to see if she was visible from where he stood. He examined every section of the store without finding her but he knew she worked there; he had seen her wearing the orange apron with the name of the store. When he applied for a job and learned that the only opening was in lumber, Chaim gratefully accepted.

Mr. Evans showed him how to use the power saw and gave him the gloves and a pair of safety goggles. Then he handed Chaim some lumber scraps and called out dimensions. As his job interview Chaim had to slice eleven chunks of timber to exact size as the assistant manager watched and approved.

Almost at once Chaim liked the sound of the power saw and the smell of wood chips. Mr. Evans trusted him with the saw, and from the first day people told him details of their lives, how many bathrooms they had or why they needed to save money by doing their own carpentry. The customers were also Chaim's teachers. Sometimes they had plans and pointed out not only their material needs but how to read their diagrams and blueprints. Because every project was new to him Chaim paid careful attention. He memorized the words they used—*fascia board*, *plywood*, *sheetrock*—and he learned to tell by observing the grain of the lumber which was the best grade.

The first week at Home Depot, Chaim earned, even after taxes and deductions, $507 and his mother announced the amount to the girls and treated Chaim as the family hero. Reb Avram also showed his pride, but Chaim felt guilty, as if he was supplanting his father, taking Avram Hirsch's place while his father was still alive and youthful and vigorous.

When there were no customers, and he had time to consider the entire domain of the lumber department, Chaim sometimes thought of Solomon, not as the great King of Israel, but as a builder, a buyer of materials, someone discussing with his advisers, as if in a biblical version of Home Depot, the best way to arrange blood drainage for the sacrifices or the proper height for the altar or the heft and quality of the timber carted down from Lebanon.

According to midrash Solomon kept 425 horses in his stable, and Chaim was attempting to figure in his head how many square feet Solomon would have needed for those horses when, from above or from beside the plywood or from heaven itself, although he knew otherwise, he heard the voice of Laura. "Hey," she said, "I know you, don't I? From Fraternity Row." She smiled. "I didn't recognize you at first, you know—I mean without your hat and stuff."

Chaim Hirsch stood numb. After all that he had observed, here she stood not two feet from his gloved hands in aisle 14. Like Chaim she wore a name tag. On his own tag he'd asked to have inscribed *Al*, since he didn't want to explain continually to the citizens of Marshall how to pronounce his name.

"Well—hi Al," she said. She stuck out her hand to greet him. Chaim removed one glove, then the other glove, then his protective eyewear. Her hand remained extended, offering friendship. It was forbidden for a Chasidic male to touch a female even casually for a handshake. His father often said, when confronted with this situation, "I shake with my heart not with my hand," but for Chaim no such phrase came to mind. He accepted her hand, reached for it, almost squeezed it in his eagerness.

"Hey," she said again—and then, "nice to meet you." She asked about plywood. On her break she was looking around thinking about building a simple bookcase. "It seems stupid to buy a bookcase when I work here, doesn't it? I don't mind just stacking my books on the floor but I've got so many it's really getting to my roommate, you know. She's getting a little weirded out."

He didn't know. The roommate he thought she meant was the one he saw her with through the fraternity's unshaded third-floor window.

But she only visited the fraternity, somewhere she had her own room and a female roommate. He'd never thought about that. It made her seem so normal. He offered to cut the wood.

"Oh, I don't have the measurements yet, just looking around. A cashier never sees anything from up front, just people in a hurry to get away. Sometimes I like to wander around on my break like a customer. If I smoked, I'd probably go outside with some of the other girls . . . It's funny you working here, too, isn't it?"

He didn't know what she meant. He put his gloves back on because Mr. Evans had warned him to do so. "Why is it funny?" he asked after pausing longer than he wished he had.

"Not really funny—a coincidence. I mean both of us working here. How long have you been here?"

"My second week," he told her.

"Do you like it?"

"Yes," he said.

She laughed and seemed to wave at him with her hair as if it was a kind of hand. "I think it's sooo bor-ing, sometimes I feel like I'll just go nuts waiting until 8:57, I'm just standing there counting the seconds. But maybe it's different back here if you're sawing and stuff. What's your favorite kind of wood?" She laughed again and leaned against a bin of dark quarter-inch paneling as if standing had taken all her energy and she needed to take a break from it. He noticed against that background the luster of her brown hair, the gray in her eyes, that she wore glasses, and a barrette, and a blue sweater with a dipping neckline, and a pin above her breast. He'd never thought of the parts of her before, never seen her as a real human being, only as a creature of his evil impulse, who performed acts to torment him because he had pulled down the black cloth and chosen to look upon unclean things.

"Come on," she teased, "you must have a favorite wood, I even have a favorite price. I like 19.99 and don't ask me why."

"Cedar," he said.

"Would that be good for a bookcase do you think?" She looked at her watch. "Can you show me some real quick? I'll come back another time with the dimensions and make sure that Jack borrows a pickup."

"We don't have any," he said, "there's some packaged cedar in the container department, I think. It's on aisle 7; people use it to keep moths away."

"Well, I don't have any moths in my books. See you later," she said. As she walked down aisle 14, Chaim knew that the truth was exactly the opposite. Later was when he would see her.

Twice a week Mindel wrote to Doctor Goodman. She read the letters first to Malka for her mother's approval. She told him about the terrible heat broken only by fierce electrical storms that sounded like the end of the world but only cooled the city for an hour. She related at length the visit of the school compliance officer, Mr. Trellis, who came right to the Hirsches' door to find out why there were five residents at this address between six and sixteen who were not going to school as the law required. She told him that her parents were afraid of the forms and the tests for the girls that had to be marked using only a number 2 pencil for the math and dark ink for the writing. But the girls were not afraid and Mr. Trellis came back himself to show Mama the scores and tell her that he wished every girl in Marshall could have this kind of home schooling with girls who knew two languages and had no desire for drugs and no worries about teen pregnancy.

"That you shouldn't write," her mother said.

"But that's what Mr. Trellis said, you heard him."

"Yes, but you don't write that in a letter."

Doctor Goodman answered twice, the first letter to apologize for having no time to write, the second time to tell her that the waiting time for an appointment with him had now stretched to two weeks although for an emergency he would always stay late. He sent regards to her family and hoped that soon she would return and that with God's help all would be well between them.

"Should I tell him that Mr. Baumgarten is feeling a little better?"

"Don't talk about Mr. Baumgarten," Malka advised. "He wants to hear about you not about a man he doesn't know."

"I have nothing more to tell him," Mindel announced. "Until we leave what else is there?"

Malka herself had corresponded with people who lived in the faraway places of America. She had cousins who had been sent on missions by the Rebbe, one to Flint, Michigan, and one to Birmingham,

Alabama, and her cousin Dovid in Arizona, who lived near the Indians. But her cousins wrote of fine people and happy community events, nothing like their own isolation in Marshall, Texas.

"We should go home and think about a wedding, not a funeral," Malka told her husband.

"I have a responsibility here, we all do," Reb Avram said. "Mr. Baumgarten didn't ask for one person but for a family. And he was right. I think he's still alive not only because he's studying Torah but because he's spending every Shabbos with us and that's what is making him stronger."

"Let him live to 120 but with another family to make him stronger," Malka said.

"We're here doing a holy mitzvah," Reb Avram said, "but we also have daughters. Think what eight dowries could mean to them."

"You're thinking about eight dowries but meanwhile if Chaim didn't work we couldn't pay one light bill."

"I know it's hard for you and for the children," Reb Avram said, "but we must have *rachmanos*. He's lived a lonely life, on the road selling to all kinds of people—he doesn't understand what it is to have a family."

When the letter marked with a red "personal only" on the envelope arrived Malka told her daughter to open it right away, but Mindel said she wanted to save it for the sabbath since it was already Friday afternoon. She left the envelope unopened, as if it was merely an advertising flyer, though she glanced at it every few minutes while she helped her mother cook and set the table. Shortly before covering her eyes for the blessing over the candles, she sliced the letter open with a knife. Malka warned the other girls not to touch it as Mindel placed the envelope near her father's prayerbook. Her sisters tried not to tease her as she put on the blue dress that she wore on Rosh Hashonah, and they granted her privacy on Saturday morning when she finally took the typewritten page into her hands to learn that the optometrist, Yossi Goodman, wished her good health and long life and hoped that she would be able in return to wish him a mazel tov upon his engagement to Elkie Frimmer, of Bensonhurst.

Mindel folded the letter and replaced it in its envelope. Her sisters roamed in and out of the living room that each Shabbos the Hirsches converted to a chapel by pushing the couch against the wall and bringing in chairs from the dining room. Mr. Baumgarten participated from the couch as Chaim and Reb Avram read from the Torah and chanted the service in Hebrew, stopping to explain whenever Mr. Baumgarten asked a question. Mindel listened to the chanting from the empty dining room while looking at herself in the mirror. She ignored her sisters' pleas to know the contents of the letter. Only after lunch and just before she left without telling anyone did Mindel whisper to Esther that "he didn't wait for me."

By four in the afternoon, when all the girls were worried, Malka told her husband what had befallen their daughter.

"Where is she?" he asked.

Reb Avram stepped out of the slippers that he had worn while preparing to take his own sabbath rest. He quickly put on his black coat and hat and his shoes and went into the street, into the crowd of fans and alumni carrying bottles and large foam fingers and electronic whistles. Reb Avram sought his daughter among the revelers. He walked quickly to the football stadium and back pushing between knots of talkers. He walked through makeshift parking lots in backyards. He searched side streets and hurried through the downtown, even checking the lobby of the Hotel Marshall to ask Eural if he had seen his daughter.

When Reb Avram returned home without Mindel, Malka said nothing. She huddled with her daughters in the kitchen as if they were already a throng of mourners. "It will be all right. Everything will be all right," he said. "Maybe it was not destined to be, that's why Hashem caused me to wait."

Malka and the girls went upstairs. "Study *Pirke Avoth* with me," he asked Chaim, but his son, looking even more stricken than the girls, said that on his one day off he had to rest and went directly to the attic. Reb Avram read from the sixth book of the Mishna alone. At the end of the sabbath he assembled the family to hear the Havdalah prayer that separates the holy day from the weekdays. Chana Tobka held the twisted candle and Esther the spice box but nobody joined Reb Avram in song. He was almost ready to call the police when long after dark Mindel returned, her hair in her eyes, her Rosh Hashonah dress looking as if she had rolled in the dirt.

Before her father could beg her forgiveness, she kissed the top of his head and from her pocket she removed and placed on the table beside him $2.54 in coins. She hugged her sisters one by one and quickly drank the juice that her tearful mother handed to her. "You can all stop crying," she said, "there's nothing wrong. Look." She pointed to the coins.

Beginning the next day, Reb Avram each morning asked Hashem to forgive his mistake and every evening he knew there was no forgiveness because Mindel spent her time walking through the campus and nearby streets, her eyes lowered, gathering, coin by coin, what she called her dowry.

Her sisters learned from her example. The youngest pulled cans and bottles out of the trash bins along Fraternity Row, then their older sisters walked with the scavengers to the supermarket to cash them in.

Reb Hirsch shook himself from attending to the dying man for one day to travel four hours by bus to Fort Worth to conduct an adult education class. Three Fort Worth residents attended. They marveled at the rabbi's knowledge but wished that he could speak more clearly and in a way that they could understand. For this service and for his careful attention to any rips in the prayer shawls and irregularities in any other ritual objects of Congregation Beth Israel, the synagogue paid Reb Hirsch two hundred dollars plus busfare; enough to keep the family equipped with electricity and gas for another month so long as they refrained from using air-conditioning. In his daily prayers Reb Hirsch gave thanks to the congregation in Fort Worth for this assistance and to the Creator of the Universe, who allowed the Hirsches to live in an area that had such a mild climate.

Finally, on the last Friday in September, four weeks after the Hirsches arrival in Marshall, Laura reappeared at the Home Depot lumber aisle. She had written the dimensions for her bookcase on a scrap of paper which she held cupped in the palm of her right hand and read aloud to Chaim the length in feet and inches as he cut, with trembling hands, to exact size. Her boyfriend, Jack, stood waiting with the lumber cart. He wore a Southern Tech cap with a long visor, which shrouded his face. Laura had asked for cedar but settled for oak. When Chaim turned off the power saw and Jack was already on his way to the checkout lanes with the cut wood, she pushed up on the balls of her feet to touch Chaim's cheek with her lips.

At the Sabbath table that evening Chaim barely paid attention to their benefactor. While the family sang the grace after meals, Mr. Baumgarten, ever more confident of the tune, rhythmically chanted the names of nearby Arkansas counties instead of Hebrew words. "Carroll and Newton," he sang out, "and Sirsi, and Yell, and Van Buren, and Cleburne, and Scott, and Sebastian."

After the singing Mr. Baumgarten felt strong enough to tell the family about his years as the buddy of Sam Walton, who had sought Baumgarten's advice and, until their final rift, had stocked Baumgarten's jewelry in the first Wal-Mart stores.

Before he started telling stories, their benefactor cleared the area in front of him by pushing the challah crumbs to his right, toward Chaim, who always sat beside the honored guest, "Maybe I should have known that Sam Walton would be a big shot someday," Mr. Baumgarten said, "but to tell you the truth, he looked to me like just another farmer in overalls a size too big. Every time that I passed through Bentonville, old Sam came out to look over this lapis necklace that he had his eye on. The man liked to haggle. Finally I gave him a big discount, who knows, maybe it was three or four dollars, or even twenty—what did it matter, the necklace wasn't really lapis anyway."

The Hirschs were amazed to learn that Mr. Walton had almost called his first Wal-Mart "the shlepper store." Mr. Baumgarten taught him the word and translated it for him and the entrepreneur liked the meaning and the sound so much that Baumgarten had to talk him out of using it. "I told him it would be an insult to the poor, to stick their nose in it by calling his place the poor man's store. Sam thought it was no disgrace to be poor and to admit it. The man had a big heart, no question that he wanted to serve the poor, that's why he became so rich. Serve the poor, that is the true road to wealth. Never forget that, son." The benefactor looked at Chaim to make his point, "Serve the poor honestly and you'll never lack a thing."

Chaim heard the words and nodded his head but as Mr. Baumgarten described the men who put down their squirrel rifles to look at jewelry in whatever town he pulled into in 1945, Chaim thought only of Laura. He wondered if at that moment she and Jack were putting together the bookcase. Even as he imagined her working with hammer and nails he couldn't stop himself from seeing her otherwise. And there was no doubt about his feelings. In the store while she and Jack talked about where in the bed of the pickup they would place the lumber, Chaim felt jealousy. It surged through him as powerfully as lust.

When Mr. Baumgarten finally released the family from the table Chaim hurried upstairs to the window of his disgrace. The room across the driveway was dark but he knew this meant nothing. Later they would turn on the dim red lamp that he had come to expect. By 11 he began to doze as he waited, but he awoke at 11:30 and again ten minutes later to see that the room remained dark.

He wondered if Laura had stayed home to put her bookcase together. He could ask her about it the next time he saw her. Maybe he would start the conversation instead of waiting for her. He might say something casual like, "Hey, how's that bookcase of yours doing?" He practiced saying it aloud quietly. This was not his way of talking, so he didn't know if it would sound natural. At the yeshiva sitting across the desk from his study partner, Itzhak, he would have been able to discuss logically whether a circumstance like his situation with Laura qualified as coveting a neighbor's wife. He might have questioned whether the fraternity man was a neighbor. Jack apparently lived in the house, but if he had not signed a lease in his own name maybe technically he wasn't a neighbor. And as to whether Laura was a wife, that Chaim doubted, although who could know? Maybe they had a certificate of marriage. That she acted the wife, of that there was no doubt. So, if she acted the wife, was she not a wife? And Chaim coveted, also without a doubt. Therefore he was in violation of the eighth commandment. The coveting, that was the violation, worse than the looking and even more impossible to stop.

The white fluorescent light across the driveway cut short his reverie. Laura stood at the window looking into the darkness. She reached to the wall to turn her lightswitch on and off several times as if testing the fixture for a defect, another subject she might talk to him about at work. In case she asked, he would check the fluorescent bulb aisle first thing on Sunday so that he would have information for her.

Her light remained off for a few minutes and then—she stood at the window again, now dressed only in her Home Depot apron. Chaim watched as she pulled it up over her waist and chest and then held the garment in front of her face as if to keep her eyes from him. Then she flicked off the lights and when she returned from darkness once more, Laura wore no apron and with closed eyes she waved to him. Chaim did not remove his gaze even when he saw in the room behind her the laughing faces of the Phi Kappa Delta boys. He looked until they, too, came to the window and waved. Only then could Chaim finally turn aside, and in that moment he understood that he would not return to the yeshiva, that these weeks in Marshall had already changed his life forever.

But even a quarter of a century later, when Chaim had strayed so far from the ways of his fathers that the Sabbath itself seemed a dream, he could not be certain whether on that last Saturday in Marshall, when in the late afternoon he had quietly closed the door of Mr. Baumgarten's house and looked into the living room toward their benefactor on the leather couch, whether he had seen his sister Mindel holding a pillow over the old man's face, or if his own acquaintance with evil had led him to imagine, even this.

Fiction Titles in the Series

Guy Davenport, *Da Vinci's Bicycle*

Stephen Dixon, *14 Stories*

Jack Matthews, *Dubious Persuasions*

Guy Davenport, *Tatlin!*

Joe Ashby Porter, *The Kentucky Stories*

Stephen Dixon, *Time to Go*

Jack Matthews, *Crazy Women*

Jean McGarry, *Airs of Providence*

Jack Matthews, *Ghostly Populations*

Jack Matthews, *Booking in the Heartland*

Jean McGarry, *The Very Rich Hours*

Steve Barthelme, *And He Tells the Little Horse the Whole Story*

Michael Martone, *Safety Patrol*

Jerry Klinkowitz, *Short Season and Other Stories*

James Boylan, *Remind Me to Murder You Later*

Frances Sherwood, *Everything You've Heard Is True*

Stephen Dixon, *All Gone: 18 Short Stories*

Jack Matthews, *Dirty Tricks*

Joe Ashby Porter, *Lithuania*

Robert Nichols, *In the Air*

Ellen Akins, *World Like a Knife*

Greg Johnson, *A Friendly Deceit*

Guy Davenport, *The Jules Verne Steam Balloon*

Guy Davenport, *Eclogues*

Jack Matthews, *Storyhood as We Know It and Other Tales*

Stephen Dixon, *Long Made Short*

Jean McGarry, *Home at Last*

Jerry Klinkowitz, *Basepaths*

Greg Johnson, *I Am Dangerous*

Josephine Jacobsen, *What Goes without Saying: Collected Stories*

Jean McGarry, *Gallagher's Travels*

Richard Burgin, *Fear of Blue Skies*

Avery Chenoweth, *Wingtips*

Judith Grossman, *How Aliens Think*

Glenn Blake, *Drowned Moon*

Robley Wilson, *The Book of Lost Fathers*

Richard Burgin, *The Spirit Returns*

Jean McGarry, *Dream Date*

Tristan Davies, *Cake*

Greg Johnson, *Last Encounter with the Enemy*

John T. Irwin and Jean McGarry, eds., *So the Story Goes: Twenty-five Years of the Johns Hopkins Short Fiction Series*

Richard Burgin, *The Conference on Beautiful Moments*

Max Apple, *The Jew of Home Depot and Other Stories*